To Kevin
From Shauna   Sept. 28/68

$1.75

THE SECRET
Tunnel Treasure

THE SECRET

ARTHUR HAMMOND

Tunnel Treasure

GENERAL EDITOR—ARTHUR HAMMOND

ILLUSTRATED BY D. JOHNSON

THE SECRET CIRCLE MYSTERIES NUMBER 4

Little, Brown and Company/Boston, Toronto

PRINTED AND BOUND BY
HAZELL WATSON AND VINEY LTD
AYLESBURY AND SLOUGH, ENGLAND

CONTENTS

1. The Treasure of Montcalm   9
2. On the Track of the Map   17
3. The Secret Message   28
4. The Isle of Sorcerers   39
5. The Shadow   51
6. A Riddle in Rhyme   62
7. Fear in the Night   72
8. Devil Worship   82
9. The Lady with the Wheel   91
10. The Graveyard Vigil   100
11. A Mysterious Disappearance   110
12. The Coiled Serpent   119
13. Where None but the Dead Should Go   128
14. Playing for Time   139
15. The Mouse Trap   150

THE SECRET
Tunnel Treasure

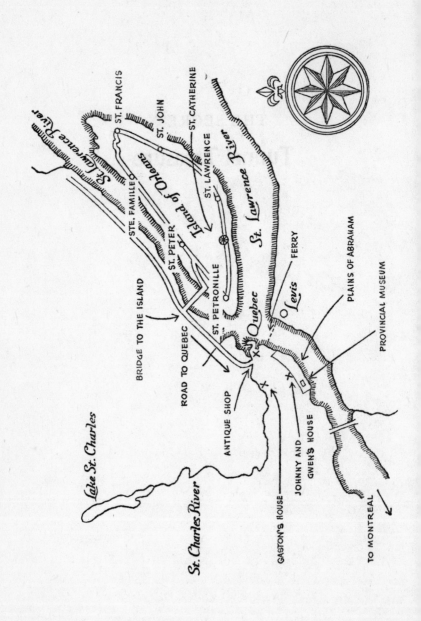

1

The Treasure of Montcalm

"Buried treasure! Right here in Quebec City! Gee, Dad, where?" Johnny Matthews bounced up and down on the arm of the chesterfield in excitement.

He might have been less pleased with the idea if he had known what that simple beginning held in store for them: for himself, for his sister Gwen, their friend Gaston, and even, finally, in those last, frightening hours, for his parents themselves. Certainly none of them would have believed, if anyone had told them, that a summer which had started so innocently was about to take a dramatic turn into high adventure; that this chance reference in a book that Mr Matthews was reading was about to lead his children off on a trail so fantastic that even their parents could not believe it—until it was almost too late.

But at the moment, none of them knew any of this, and Johnny's question still hung in the air unanswered.

It was his mother who answered first.

"I'll gee Dad you, if you don't stop bouncing around on that furniture," she said, looking up from her sewing. "How on earth did you get your shirt in this mess, anyway?" She held it up to the lamp, showing everyone the large, triangular rip in the sleeve.

"It was the Mouse, Mom," his sister Gwen said, leaning over the back of her father's chair. "He was teasing the Mouse, and it tore his shirt."

Anyone who didn't know the family would have thought that Gwen was crazy to talk about mice tearing people's shirts, but Mrs Matthews just grunted and Mr Matthews went on reading without even looking up. It seemed quite normal to them, because the Mouse was the family dog, who at this very moment was showing how he had got his name by hiding underneath the chesterfield with only his nose showing, in a place which you wouldn't have thought was big enough for a mouse, let alone a dog. Whenever it looked as if there were going to be trouble, he headed for the smallest hole he could find and squeezed himself in, which was what he was doing now, his shining eyes shifting uneasily in the dark, from the shirt to Johnny and back again.

However, Mrs Matthews just sighed and went on sewing, and the Mouse allowed his nose to emerge just an inch or two more into the lamplight.

Johnny screwed up his face at his sister and stuck out his tongue. "Yah, tattletale."

And not being able to think of anything better for the moment, Gwen did just the same back at him, over the top of her father's head. "Yah, tattletale."

Her father's hand reached up behind him and, without even looking up from his book, he managed to find her nose and squeeze it gently between his thumb and finger.

"Now, do you two want to hear this story or not?" he said.

"Yes, Daddy, yes," Gwen said, trying to pull herself free from his fingers.

"Yes, Dad, what about this buried treasure? Whose was it, a pirate or someone's?"

Mr Matthews finally looked up from his book. "A pirate or someone's?" he said in amazement. "John Matthews, did you or did you not go to school last year?"

Johnny nodded.

"Then will you tell me exactly what *pirates* would be doing around Quebec City?"

Johnny looked down at his feet. It was just terrible having a history teacher for a father. He always knew all the answers. Gwen giggled.

"You shut up," Johnny said. "You don't know either."

"I do so. There weren't any pirates around Quebec City."

"Thank you, Gwen," her father said. "I'm glad that some member of this family has been paying attention to her poor overworked teachers at school. Now, John Matthews—you tell me what the most exciting thing that ever happened in Quebec City was."

Johnny thought carefully, suspecting a trap. He looked at the Mouse for help. The Mouse slowly withdrew his nose again.

"Was it about General Wolfe?" Johnny said hesitantly.

"It was indeed about General Wolfe," his father said. "And what did General Wolfe do?"

"He captured Quebec from the French," Johnny said more confidently.

"Good. In 1759, just over two hundred years ago, General Wolfe captured Quebec from General Montcalm, who was in charge of the French army here."

There was a faint sigh of relief from Johnny. The Mouse, too, sensing that the questions were over, stuck his head out again and seemed to grin, his tongue lolling out of the side of his mouth.

"Well, now that we've got that cleared up," Mr Matthews said, smiling, "I'll read you this story. You know that Quebec had been an important city long before General Wolfe ever came and attacked it. There were many rich merchants here who traded with the Indians for their furs and then sent them back to France to sell. And then in France they would buy expensive and valuable things to be sent back here: silver and sometimes gold plate for their houses and jewels for their wives. The churches had lots of valuable ornaments too, and so did many of the officers and nobles of the garrison, including General Montcalm himself. Well, when the inhabitants knew that the British were sailing up the river to attack them, many of them naturally began to think about hiding all this treasure somewhere. The British might actually succeed in capturing the city and then seize everything they found inside it. This is what the book says about it:

"The legend says that the whole plan was then entrusted to the General, who had a secret hiding place prepared which only he and one of his trusted officers knew about. The soldiers of the garrison who were employed on the project were always taken to the place blindfolded, and by a roundabout route, so that no one but the two men in charge could ever know where the

hiding place was. In this way they could be sure that none of their own side would be tempted to steal the treasure or be able to tell the British its whereabouts even if they wanted to.

"Finally, when word came that the British were close to the city, the treasure of Montcalm was taken out secretly, at night, by the General and his officer, and hidden. The idea was that if the British were defeated, the treasure could be brought back into the city, but that if the city fell, it could be carried away to France and reclaimed there by its owners.

"Then the British came and the city was captured, but in the battle something happened which no one had foreseen. Both General Montcalm and the officer he had trusted were killed, so that no one was left who knew the whereabouts of the treasure. Afterwards, many of the French inhabitants made searches about the city, especially along the banks of the St Charles River, where the treasure was rumoured to be hidden, but no trace was ever found of it, and eventually the story was forgotten. Now only the legend remains that before the capture of Quebec a great treasure was smuggled out of the city and hidden, in some place where it has never been found."

Mr Matthews closed the book and looked round at his silent audience.

Johnny leaned towards him on the arm of the chesterfield, which he was riding like a horse. "Gee, Dad," he said. "Supposing we could find it! Wouldn't that be something?"

His father reached over and rapped him sharply on the head with his book. "It would indeed be something.

For one thing we'd be able to afford to buy a new chester-field for the people who own this house, after you've finished pulling the arms off that one. Sit on it properly."

Johnny slid down off the arm with a sigh. That was the trouble with grown-ups. Here was a whole buried treasure, right underneath their feet maybe, and they made a fuss about how you sat on a chesterfield. No sense of proportion.

"But, Daddy, didn't they even leave a map or any-thing?" Gwen said. "They must have known that they might get killed and that then no one would know where the treasure was."

"That's all it says here, Gwen. Remember, this whole story is only a rumour. There may never have been any treasure at all."

"I bet there was," Johnny said. "You know what I would have done if I'd been Montcalm and knew that the enemy was going to attack at any moment? I'd have taken the treasure out at dead of night and buried it, and then I'd have shot the officer who had helped me, so that no one could ever tell the tale. I bet that's what happened. I bet old Montcalm actually shot the other guy and buried his corpse with the treasure." Johnny held up his hand like a pistol and fired twice, once into the officer's back, and then again as he fell. "Pow! Pow!" Then he started to make shovelling motions.

"All right, Captain Blood, maybe that's what you'd do," his father said, laughing. "But maybe General Montcalm hadn't seen quite as much TV or read quite as many comics as you have."

"But, Daddy, wouldn't they have made a map? Wouldn't they?" Gwen said.

"I don't know, my dear. Maybe they would have. It certainly seems a sensible enough thing to do."

"Well, then, all we've got to do is find the map, and then we'll find the treasure," Johnny said.

"And how exactly do you propose to go about finding the map?" his father said, laughing. "I should have thought that that would be about as hard as finding the treasure itself."

"No, maybe there's a map, but nobody knew it was a treasure map, so they didn't pay any attention to it. There must be lots of old maps around that Montcalm had and nobody's ever paid any attention to, because they didn't know they were of any importance. If we could find old Montcalm's old maps, maybe we could find the right one."

The Mouse stuck his head out farther from under the chesterfield and cocked his ears at the excitement in Johnny's voice. This sort of voice usually meant adventure of some kind. He looked up expectantly and began to scrabble at the floor trying to get out.

"Get that dog out from under there and put him outside for the night," his mother said, looking up. "It's time for bed."

Johnny ignored her for the moment. "Where could we find some old maps, Dad? Where are Montcalm's old maps?"

His father smiled. "I don't know. I suppose you could try the Provincial Museum and see what they've got. I don't think you'll find any treasure, but you might learn a little history and that won't do you any harm."

The scrabbling noise became louder, more frantic. The Mouse was stuck.

"Did you hear what I said?" his mother said. "Get that dog out from under there and start getting ready for bed."

Johnny heaved at the chesterfield and lifted it slightly. Suddenly released, the Mouse shot across the floor in a tangle of rugs and then stood up wagging his tail, very pleased at how easily he had got out. Johnny led him out the back door into the garden, then went back and said good night to his parents thoughtfully and went upstairs.

Gwen was waiting for him on the landing. The house the Matthews had rented for the summer, while Mr Matthews took a summer course at Laval University, was on the Avenue de Bernières, overlooking the Plains of Abraham and the river. The St Lawrence was silver in the distance, sparkling in the light of an almost full moon. Up this river, two hundred years before, had come Wolfe and his redcoats, and out that same way, perhaps, had slipped two men, carrying the treasure of Montcalm. Somewhere in the city, he decided, was the clue to its whereabouts, and tomorrow they would start to track it down.

Somewhere in the city, too, but unknown to Johnny, were people who had other plans.

2

On the Track of the Map

The next morning, much to everyone's surprise, Johnny was up and dressed even before his mother went in to call him. Usually, especially in schooltime, he was so hard to get out of bed that she had to pull all the bedclothes off him before he would move. Now, when she came to pour him out his glass of orange juice at the breakfast table, she put her hand on his forehead to feel his temperature.

"Johnny Matthews, are you all right?" she said with a smile.

"Of course I'm all right, Mom. We've just got to get on the track of that map, that's all. What time does that museum open up that you told us about, Dad?"

His father looked up from the paper. "You'll have plenty of time for that," he said. "The doors don't open until ten o'clock. You'll be the earliest customer they ever had."

Johnny looked at the clock. Ten after eight. "Aw gee, Dad," he moaned. "That's hours yet!"

"That's fine," his mother said, putting down his plate of cereal in front of him. "That'll give you and Gwen just nice time to do one or two chores for me before you go rushing off for the day."

Johnny looked across at Gwen, who had just sat down at the table, and they groaned in unison.

But even so, well before ten o'clock, they were both sitting on the grass, near their bicycles, outside the Provincial Museum, which was quite close to where they lived, on the Plains of Abraham. They were throwing a stick for the Mouse to retrieve, and were being closely watched by a boy who had arrived a little after them and was now sitting near his bicycle at the foot of the museum steps. Finally, one time when the Mouse had run close to him and was worrying the stick, he called to the dog and it went over to investigate him, wagging its tail. The boy took the stick.

"Allez! Apporte, Fido!" he shouted, throwing it, and the Mouse, who seemed to understand French perfectly, rushed off madly after it again.

Johnny decided that they had better show him that the dog belonged to them, so he got up and walked over beside him, with Gwen following.

"That dog's name is Mouse," he said.

"Mows?" the boy said seriously. "Why do you call him mows when he is a dog?"

"It's just a name," Gwen explained. "He gets stuck in holes, like a mouse."

The boy smiled. "Ah, he gets stuck in holes." Then he laughed.

"What did you yell at him then when you threw the stick?" Johnny said.

"I just told him to fetch the stick," the boy said. "You don't speak French?"

"No," Gwen said. "They don't teach it to us in school yet. But you speak English."

"Oh, *oui*, yes. In my school we learn it, and my father, he speaks it. He is a *fonctionnaire*—how do you call it? —a civil servant."

"Our father is a teacher—a history teacher," Gwen said. "He can speak French."

"And he doesn't teach you?"

"We don't have to speak French," Johnny explained. "Everyone where we come from speaks English."

The Mouse had finally come back with the stick again, panting. Johnny took it and threw it.

"I don't have to speak English, too," the boy said, "if I don't want to." He sounded a little angry. "I am a Canadian."

"Everybody's a Canadian," Johnny said, getting mad himself because the other boy sounded mad. "Canada's an English country."

"It is *not* an English country!" the boy shouted. "Quebec is a French country. You English are stupid, thinking you own everything!"

"Who's English, stupid?" Johnny yelled back. "I didn't mean that. I meant everyone in Canada had to *speak* English."

They stood glaring at each other.

"I do not have to speak English," the boy said.

"Yes, you do," Johnny said. "It's the law. We beat you."

"What is that, you beat us?" the boy said, breathing heavily.

"General Wolfe beat you," Johnny yelled. "He licked you."

Suddenly the boy lunged at Johnny and pushed him over on the grass. "You don't lick nobody!" he shouted. "General Wolfe was helped by traitors."

Johnny grabbed the boy's legs and pulled him down and they began to roll over and over, punching each other and wrestling. Gwen began to jump up and down, shouting "Stop it! Stop it!" and the Mouse began to run round and round them, barking and jumping in at them. They took no notice. They fought on until they were both exhausted and then suddenly sat back on the grass and looked at each other. Johnny's nose was bleeding slightly and the other boy was gingerly feeling a loose tooth. The Mouse came up and sniffed at them both, then started wagging his tail. Johnny suddenly noticed that Gwen had gone.

"Where's my sister?" he said.

The other boy looked round. "I don't know."

At that moment they saw her. The side door of the museum had opened and she was coming out of it now with one of the attendants, who was wearing a blue uniform. She pointed at the boys and they looked at each other and got up.

"I'll kill her if she's been telling tales," Johnny said.

"I will talk to him," the boy said. "He is probably French."

But when the attendant came up to them, although he did have a French accent, he spoke in English.

"It's all right," Johnny said, not looking at the other boy. "We've made it up."

"Ah, so," the attendant said, turning to the other boy.

"*Oui*," the boy said, and then the attendant began to talk to him very rapidly in French. Johnny didn't under-

stand what he was saying, but he knew that the boy was being bawled out.

"It's not his fault," he said. "It's mine. I started it."

The attendant looked at him. "Ah, so," he said again. "Then you will kindly shake hands and become friends." He stood looking at them, waiting. "What are your names?"

"Gaston," the boy said, holding out his hand.

"Johnny," Johnny said, shaking it.

"And I'm Gwen," Gwen said.

"Good!" the attendant said. "Now, if you wish to see the museum—you will kindly come in and not fight."

Johnny ordered the Mouse to wait outside. Then, as they walked in the side entrance, he said to the man, "We just want to see some old maps, please. Maps that General Montcalm had, if you've got any."

The man looked at him curiously and then led them through a little lobby into a room lined on both sides with bookcases reaching up to the ceiling, like a library.

"But first," the man said, "you must sign our Visitors' Book. We like to have the name and address of everyone who visits us."

He produced a ball-point pen and a large, heavy, dark-covered volume, and they each wrote in their name and address before looking round at the room more carefully.

Down the centre ran a long glass-topped display case, with various objects and documents inside. Hanging on its sides were a number of old glass-framed maps. The attendant pointed to these as he looked up from reading their signatures.

"*Voilà*," he said. "There are plenty of old maps."

Johnny hesitated. "Did any of these actually belong to General Montcalm?" he said. "Those are the ones we want to see."

"Ah, General Montcalm," the attendant said, with a shrug, staring at him. "No, those are not his maps. What is it you want with General Montcalm?"

Gwen started to say something about the treasure but Johnny interrupted her quickly.

"Oh well, we'll have a look at these anyway," he said, drawing her away. "We were just interested." He began to walk off down the room, with Gwen and Gaston following him. The man had looked much too interested at the mention of treasure. They would have to be careful whom they told things to.

Johnny stopped in front of the first map that was hanging up and looked at it, then gave a little gasp of annoyance. "Look at this," he said to Gwen. "We're just crazy!"

She came up beside him and looked at the map. "What's wrong with it?" she said. "Why are we crazy?"

"Look at it," he said in an annoyed voice. "It's in French. And so would General Montcalm's maps be. We couldn't even understand them if we found them!"

Gwen stared at the map for a few moments in silence. Johnny was quite right. Then suddenly she had an idea.

"But Gaston could understand them!" she said. "Why don't we let Gaston in on the secret, and then he can help us out?"

"What is all this about General Montcalm?" Gaston said. "And what is this secret and this treasure you mentioned just now? This is a map of the old city of Quebec. Look, I will show you," and he went over it, reading out the names of the streets and buildings to them in English and explaining things.

Johnny looked at him for a moment and then at his sister, who nodded her head vigorously.

"Yes, go on, Johnny," she said. "Let's tell him."

"All right," Johnny said. "Look, Gaston—I'm sorry about that fight we had. I guess I just lost my temper."

"No, it was my fault," Gaston said quietly. "You are a visitor to our province. I should have kept *my* temper."

"Well, anyway," Gwen burst out, unable to contain herself any longer, "we've discovered that there's buried treasure somewhere around this city, and we've got an idea that there must be a map somewhere which will show us where to find it."

"Look," Johnny said uneasily, looking round about him. "Let's go outside and talk about this." The attendant, who seemed to be rather suspicious of what they might be up to, had moved closer to them again and was dusting one of the glass cases.

As they walked down the room past him, he looked up from his work and stared at them, then began to follow them slowly down the room. As they walked out to where the Mouse was sitting waiting for them by their bicycles, the man came out and stood in the doorway, looking after them.

"A treasure?" Gaston said suspiciously, as soon as they were out in the open, beyond where the man could hear them. "What kind of a treasure?"

"Our father has an old book which says that General Montcalm buried some treasure before he was beaten by General Wol. . . ." Gwen saw the look coming into Gaston's eye again. "Well, anyway, before he was killed, that is," she added hurriedly. "And Daddy says it has never been discovered."

"Ah, yes—the treasure of Montcalm," Gaston said. "My grandfather has told me about this, but nobody really believes that it exists."

"That's right," Johnny said excitedly. "Our father doesn't really seem to think it exists either, but we think there may be a map somewhere which would show us the way to it. Montcalm wouldn't have gone out to battle without leaving some clue to it, would he?"

Gaston thought for a moment. "Then this is why you are looking for the maps of General Montcalm in the museum?"

They looked round, but the attendant had disappeared from the doorway, apparently satisfied that they had not stolen anything.

"Yes, that's right," Gwen said. "Daddy said it might be a good place to start to look."

"Ah, but that is no good," Gaston said. "If they had such a map in the museum, they would know at once what it was and would have found the treasure for themselves. The things of Montcalm in the museum have been studied and studied by everyone. If there is a map, we must look for it somewhere else."

"Then you *will* help us?" Gwen said, clasping her hands together in excitement.

"But of course," Gaston said. "This treasure belongs to us—to the people of Quebec—and I can help to bring it back."

"Now just a minute," Johnny said, beginning to get angry again.

"Oh, do stop it, you two!" Gwen said. "There'll be

plenty for everyone if we find it. But we've all got to work together. Let's make a pact to be equal partners."

"Very well. But it must be a blood pact," Gaston said. "Only a blood pact is enough."

"A blood pact!" Gwen squeaked. "You mean we've got to sign our names in blood?"

"No, stupid!" Johnny said. "We just mix some of our blood together." He began fumbling in his pockets, looking for a pin.

"I have a knife," Gaston said, producing a small clasp-knife from his pocket and opening a tiny blade on it. "It is very sharp, this blade."

"You're not going to cut us all with a knife?" Gwen asked faintly. "I won't do it. I'll swear on the Bible instead."

"It's just a pinprick, silly," Johnny said. "Hold out your arm."

"No, I won't do it. Johnny, you're not to touch me," she said, backing away.

"Then it is no good," Gaston said, shrugging his shoulders. "Unless we are willing to give blood for each other, it is no good."

Gwen looked at the two of them, Gaston glum, and Johnny angry. Boys! Always talking about blood! Why couldn't they just shake hands? She clenched her teeth and held out her arm. "All right—but don't hurt me."

She closed her eyes and Gaston gave her arm the faintest prick with the point of the knife, then did his own and Johnny's. Johnny touched his finger to the three little drops of blood and mixed them together, putting a dab on each arm.

"Now the oath," Gaston said. "I, Gaston St Hilaire . . ."

"And I, John Malcolm Matthews . . ."

"And I, Gwendolyn Janet Matthews . . ."

". . . solemnly swear to help my blood brothers in the search for the treasure of Montcalm," Gaston went on, "and to share with them the dangers and rewards, as far as death itself."

"I swear," they all said together. Gwen giggled.

Johnny glared at her. "Where do we start looking for this map if it isn't in the museum?" he said to Gaston.

"I have an idea." Gaston said. "Follow me."

3

The Secret Message

Where Gaston led them was to an antique shop, the first of a series which they visited during the next week or so asking for old maps and then looking at any that the owners of the stores had to show them. They had decided that they would say they were looking for one as a present for Johnny's father, whose birthday was coming soon, so that no one would get suspicious and begin to think they were looking for something valuable.

They were very discouraged when they had no luck at first and so they decided that they would visit only one shop a day, to prevent themselves from becoming bored with the search. And they agreed that they would keep on that way, whenever they had time, until they had visited every old junk shop and antique shop in the area.

They visited shops in the old city on top of the hill, and shops outside the city walls, down in the newer part near the station. They looked at maps of Canada and maps of the world, maps in English and maps in French, old maps and new maps, until they were almost dizzy with looking at maps. But still they had found nothing that looked even faintly like a treasure map that might have been left behind by General Montcalm.

And so it was that the next Friday found them leaning, feeling rather discouraged, on one of the old black cannons at their usual meeting place on the ramparts, looking down at the river and the roofs of Lower Town directly below them.

"Gee, I don't know," Johnny said gloomily. "Maybe it's useless. We must have visited every old antique shop in the city by now and we haven't found a thing."

Gaston leaned against the mouth of the cannon with a frown of concentration, watching one of the ferries to Lévis on the other side of the river, curving out against the current.

"No!" he said suddenly. "I know where there is one that we haven't tried, and a good one too." He slapped himself on the forehead. "Why didn't I remember that yet? It's quite close to here too."

"Okay. Let's go," Johnny said, pushing himself up off the cannon. "But if we don't have any luck this time I think I'll be about ready to give up altogether."

Gaston led them along the ramparts, past the long line of old cannons and mortars, and then, carrying their bicycles, down a steep flight of metal steps which ran down the cliff into Lower Town. In front of them was one of the typical old streets, full of tall stone houses and shops, running down to the harbour.

"This is *Sous le Fort*," Gaston said, "Under the Fort. Here is an old shop which I should have remembered before. I was there once with my father when he was looking for a special present for someone. This owner even collects maps. I remember he asked my father if he had any to sell. But he is a strange one, this owner. Even my father says so. My father told me that the police have suspected him of being—how do you say?— someone who buys the stolen goods. But they have never caught him."

Gaston led them a little way down the street to where the shop was, its dirty old window full of the most incredible jumble of furniture, paintings, china, books, and weapons that they had seen yet. They peered into the gloomy interior and then climbed the two steps to the door and pushed in.

Inside, the room was very dark and it was piled from floor to ceiling with every kind of object you could imagine. There were suits of armour, African spears, about two dozen chandeliers of all shapes and sizes hanging from the ceiling and covered in cobwebs, tables and chairs and wardrobes, an anchor, some old muskets, a carved wooden arm sticking out from the wall with a candle-holder in its hand, an elephant's foot umbrella stand, a stuffed white bulldog with one ear chewed off —which the Mouse went up to and sniffed curiously— and, in one corner, hanging from a wire, a skeleton.

"Oh!" Gwen said with a little jump.

"That, my dear," said a thin voice behind her, "is George. Were you thinking of buying him?"

"Oh no, it's horrible! I mean, no thank you," Gwen said hurriedly.

"And yet he was a very kindly man when he lived. Fond of children," the man said. "And of dogs. And now the dogs are fond of him." He pointed with a long thin finger at the Mouse, who had moved on from the mysteriously unfriendly bulldog and was now looking

thoughtfully at the skeleton. His tongue came out and licked his lips. The man smiled unpleasantly.

"Mouse, come here!" Gwen said sharply. The Mouse gave her a hurt look, glanced regretfully at the skeleton, licked his lips again, and then came over and sat down.

"We were looking for some old maps," Johnny said, looking at the man uneasily. He was tall and stooped, with a long thin face and absolutely no hair, and when he smiled he showed long, yellow teeth. In the dusk of the shop he looked more than a little menacing.

"Ah, maps," he said, rubbing his thin hands together, and then again, "ah, so you are looking for maps, are you?" He stared at them for a moment in silence, as if calculating something, and then went on, beginning to rub his hands together again. "Yes, we have plenty of maps. Old maps, new maps, big maps, small maps, maps of the earth and maps of the moon. Maybe even . . . a few treasure maps." He looked from one to the other of them, watching them closely, and bared his teeth again in his thin smile.

Johnny looked at Gaston in alarm. Treasure maps! Was the man a mind-reader or something? It was impossible, and yet he seemed to know exactly what they were thinking. Or was it just one of his jokes, a lucky, chance remark?

Gaston shook his head at Johnny behind the store-keeper's back, as the man turned to lead them towards the back of the long store, through the maze of old furniture and antiques. He didn't know what to make of the remark either.

They stopped at the very back of the store, in front of a small table absolutely covered with maps. They were piled in cardboard boxes, with other heaps of loose maps scattered all around. There were hundreds—more maps than they had seen at all the other stores put together.

The man waved his hand over the table. "Was there any particular kind of map you wanted?" he said very loudly, making them jump. "You see, we have quite a few. They're something of a hobby of mine. One never knows what one will find." He smiled again, watching them closely.

"No, we just wanted one for our father's birthday," Johnny said. "We'd just like to have a look through them."

"I see. For your father's birthday." The man grinned at them more mirthlessly than ever. "Perhaps he would have one or two maps he could show me? I could give him a good price for the right article. A good price." He looked from one to the other of them.

"Oh no," Johnny said, taking a deep breath. "He hasn't got very many. Only one or two as a matter of fact, and I know he wants to keep them."

He wished the man would go away and leave them to look at the maps in peace, though he was beginning to lose hope that they would find anything here that this man had missed.

But finally, after another short silence, the man did turn to go. "I see," he said again, his voice quieter now, as if he were talking to himself. "Then I'll leave you here to search for what you want." He gave his widest smile of all, and then added, "Do take care of your little dog. I wouldn't want him wandering off and ending up like our stuffed bulldog at the front. Would you?" And then he turned and walked away in the shadows towards the front of the shop.

"I told you he is a strange one," Gaston said, after he had disappeared. "Even my father says so after we came in here."

"Strange! I think he's kooky," Gwen said. "I don't think it's safe in here." She reached down and grabbed the Mouse. "I'm going to take him outside before something happens to him."

"Don't be crazy," Johnny said. "He was kidding you. He just doesn't want the Mouse wandering about and breaking things, that's all. Tie him to something. Here."

He pulled the Mouse's long leash out of his pocket and clipped it onto his collar. Then he looked round and heaved up one corner of a heavy table so that Gwen could slip the noose end of the leash round the table leg. When he let the leg down again, the Mouse was safely tethered, though he could wander around at the end of his leash within sight. Then they turned to the maps, looking at them closely in the dim light of the shop.

Johnny picked up a handful and dropped them again. "Gee," he said, "we'll never get through all these. It'll take us all day."

"We can divide them up," Gaston said. "You do that end of the table, and I will do this end, and Gwen can do the middle."

"Okay," Johnny said. "And we can go pretty quickly, because we know what kind of map we're looking for. It'll be in French, and it'll be of Quebec City or the country just around, so we can ignore anything like this old map of the world," he said, putting it aside. "And it'll be on old paper or parchment and probably not very big. Those are our clues."

They began to work.

The shop remained strangely silent. The shopkeeper didn't come back to speak to them again, but every now and again Johnny got the feeling that they were being watched, and once or twice they heard a faint noise, as if someone had shifted his feet or moved a chair somewhere near them. There was a door at the very back of the shop, which seemed to lead to a living-room, or perhaps a store room, and above the door was a small rectangular window of dim glass, of the kind one sometimes finds in old houses. Johnny had an idea that the sounds came from there and he looked up suddenly several times to see if he could catch anyone watching them through the glass. But if there was anyone there, they were too quick for him, for he could see no sign of movement. And finally he decided that it must just be his nerves playing tricks on him and he bent over his maps, without bothering to look up again. But all the time he could feel the window looking down on him, almost as if it were a dim yellow eye with a life of its own.

He could have ended the suspense by walking over and pulling the door open, to see if there was anyone behind it, but that was more than he dared do. What if it were only some member of the shopkeeper's family? What excuse could he give them for bursting into their living-room? And if it were someone else, someone who was indeed listening to them, perhaps spying on them through the glass above the door? What could he do even if he discovered them? No, best to go on working and keep their voices low.

But he had no need to tell the others. The spooky atmosphere of the store had gradually begun to affect them, too, and when they spoke to each other now, they spoke in whispers.

After a while had passed, with no sound except the rustle of the maps as they turned them over, Gwen groaned and straightened her back.

"I think this is hopeless," she whispered. "And if we stay here much longer, that kooky old man is going to come back to see what we're up to. We're never going to find it."

Gaston was despondent too. "Perhaps it was foolish to hope so," he said. "After so many years, when so many other people didn't find it, why should we?"

But Johnny just gritted his teeth. He had already begun to give up hope too, but it had been his idea to look for a map in the first place and, whatever he might say, he was going to go through with it until they had searched every antique shop and old junk shop in the city.

Suddenly Gwen noticed that the Mouse had been very quiet for a long time, and looked round to see what he was doing. To her amazement, he was gone.

"Where's the Mouse gone?" she whispered urgently, with visions of finding him already stuffed and standing out in the front of the shop with the chewed-up bulldog.

The others looked round. "The leash's still there," Johnny said, looking at it in amazement. It ran from the table leg, where they had looped it, across the floor and into a small black leather trunk. The lid of the trunk was tightly closed!

"What on earth . . . ?" Johnny got up and stepped over

to the trunk. There was a catch on the lid, but it was unlocked and he lifted the lid easily. Inside, curled comfortably asleep on a bed of old books, lay the Mouse. Now he woke up, opened his mouth in a wide yawn, and began wagging his tail as well as he could in such a small space. Then he stood up, stretched, yawned again and jumped out, as if there were really nothing very remarkable about a dog of his intelligence being able to get inside a closed trunk.

"It must have been open just a little bit," Gwen said, "so that he could squeeze his nose in. That's just the kind of thing he loves. Then he must have climbed in and it must have fallen shut behind him. Maybe that was one of the noises we heard. It's leather. It wouldn't make much noise."

Johnny opened the lid a little and then dropped it. It closed almost without a sound.

"He really is a mows," Gaston said, laughing.

Johnny reached into the trunk and pulled out one of the books. "What's he been using for a pillow?" he said. It was an old leather-bound volume, thick with dust and printed in French. It looked as if rats had been chewing at the edges. He flipped through a few pages, wrinkling his nose at the dust, and then handed it to Gaston.

"*Sermons de Monseigneur Philippe de Brébeuf. Tome un,*" Gaston read. "Sermons of My Lord Philip of Brébeuf. Volume one."

Johnny was looking at the other books. "Sermon's the same word in English and French, isn't it?" he said. "These are all sermons. Gee, what a lot of dull books. No wonder no one ever bothered to take them out of the trunk even." He went on looking at them briefly and piling them on the floor one by one. Gwen sneezed from the cloud of dust.

Suddenly they were interrupted by a hiss from Gaston, who had been looking at the first book. "Listen to this," he whispered. "Here is a sermon in this book about treasure. It is called," he hesitated over the translation, " 'The Kingdom of Heaven is like treasure hidden in a field.' "

"I know that," Gwen said. "That's from the Bible."

"But listen!" Gaston went on excitedly. "When I turned to the page to look at this sermon, look what I found." He held the book out for them to look at. There, in between the lines of print, was writing in a small neat hand, the ink brown and faded with age.

"Yes, but what does it say?" Johnny asked, his voice suddenly quiet. The air in their dark corner of the shop was suddenly electric with excitement.

"I don't know," Gaston said. "It is too faint. I can't read it in this light. But look again." He turned over a few more pages in the book. At the end of each sermon there was a blank page of white paper. And on the blank page after the sermon about treasure, drawn in the same faded old brown ink, was something that made all their hearts miss a beat. A map.

4

The Isle of Sorcerers

"What does it say there on the map, Gaston?" Gwen said. "It must be an explanation of some kind."

Gaston looked at the map closely. "It is very difficult to see," he said. "It is so faint. It is an island, and it has got these crosses marked on it, and then some words. Let's see. '*L'Île*.' That's the same word 'isle,' or 'island.' '*Des Sorc . . . ières*.' Yes, that's it, '*L'Île des Sorcières*'— 'the Isle of Sorcerers.' And then, underneath, it says '*où nous avons caché le nôtre*'—'where we have hidden ours.' "

"Crikey!" Gwen said. "Sorcerers! Wherever's that?"

Before Gaston could reply, Johnny reached over and grabbed the book from him, slamming it shut.

"Hey!" Gaston said angrily.

"It doesn't matter," Johnny said loudly. "I'd rather get this for Dad." He gave Gaston a warning look and then looked past him, over his shoulder. Gaston and Gwen looked round, and the owner of the store stepped towards them out of the shadows, rubbing his hands.

"Ah, so you've found something, have you?" he said, looking from one to the other with his unpleasant smile.

Johnny hesitated, wondering how much the man had heard and how long he had been standing in the shadows. He decided to try to bluff it out.

"Yes," he said. "We decided not to get him a map after all. We'll get one of these old books." He didn't give the man the book he was holding but pointed to the pile they had made on the floor. The man looked down and then stooped and picked one up.

While he was looking at it, Johnny put down the book he was holding and picked up another one, as if he was still deciding which one they were going to buy. Whatever happened, he didn't want the man to look at the book that had the map in it. If he saw that, and the writing, he would never sell it to them. So Johnny picked up a second book and then a third, gradually hiding the first one in the pile.

The shopkeeper looked up at him suspiciously. "This is a very strange change from a map," he said. "These are old books of sermons."

"I know," Johnny said. "But my father loves reading old sermons. It's his hobby. He collects old books of sermons too. This is the kind of thing he'll love for his birthday. He might even come back and buy some of the others if we tell him where we got this one."

Gwen looked away uneasily, and shuffled her feet. It was an awful lie, and even Johnny didn't know if anyone would ever believe it, but it was the only thing he could think of on the spur of the moment. The shop-keeper looked at him and frowned. He obviously didn't find it very easy to swallow. But, on the other hand, he couldn't see any reason why they shouldn't buy an old book of sermons if they wanted to.

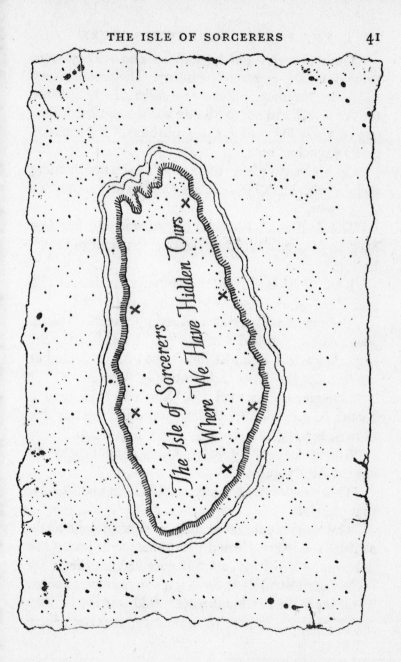

The Isle of Sorcerers — Where We Have Hidden Ours

"These are very old books," he said. "They were printed in the eighteenth century. They're not very valuable, but they're quite expensive simply because they're so old. I'm not at all sure you'd be able to afford one of these for your father's birthday." He sounded really suspicious now.

"Oh, we've got plenty of money," Gwen said, coming to Johnny's aid. "Our mother's going to help us pay for the present."

The shopkeeper looked at her suspiciously, and then back at Johnny. "Which is the one you want to buy?" he said.

Johnny hesitated. "We haven't quite decided yet," he said. "Would all these books be the same price?"

The man bent over and picked up several of them. Johnny's heart missed a beat. Now he was holding the book they wanted. But he didn't open it, just looked at the backs of the books and put them down again.

"I imagine so," the man said. "Much the same, though I can't be sure till I see the one you want. But any one of these is going to cost you at least thirty dollars."

"Thirty dollars!" Johnny, Gwen, and Gaston all gasped aloud together.

"Thirty dollars for one old book!" Gwen said. "Golly, that's terrible!"

The shopkeeper was smiling his strange smile again as if he were very pleased with some secret joke. "My dear young lady," he said. "If your father collects old books you must surely know that it's an expensive hobby. These books are two hundred years old, and even if they aren't particularly rare or interesting, their age alone makes them worth more than that. At thirty dollars each, they're an extraordinary bargain."

"Of course they are," Johnny said hurriedly, afraid that their surprise would give the game away. "Dad's paid hundreds of dollars for a book sometimes."

The shopkeeper was beginning to pick up the books and look at them again, and so Johnny reached for them and said, "Could we just have a look at these again for a minute, to decide whether this is really the best thing to get for him?"

"Certainly," the man said, giving them to him. "I'll be at the front of the store when you've made up your minds. I don't think you'll want all these, will you?" he added, picking up the pile from the floor. "They need a little dusting." He turned and walked away, carrying the pile of books against his chest.

"It's all right," Johnny whispered, as soon as he was out of sight. "He hasn't got the one with the map. I was keeping my eye on it." He pulled out one of the books he was holding and put the others down. "Here it is— *Sermons de Monseigneur Philippe de Brébeuf. Tome un.*" His imitation of Gaston's accent was quite good and they all smiled.

"Good," Gaston said. "You are learning some French."

But Johnny, instead of replying, suddenly spun round and looked at the door at the back of the store. Had he heard it close? There had been the faintest click, like a latch falling into place. If it had been ajar all this time . . . !

The others turned and followed his eyes, looking alarmed, and suddenly he made up his mind. This had got to be settled once and for all. He walked around the few pieces of furniture that stood between him and the door, reached it, and then hesitated with his hand on the latch. Then he pushed the latch down silently and pulled the door open.

His heart missed a beat, and then he stared in.

Nothing.

It was a small sitting-room, which the store owner also obviously used as an office. A desk on one side was covered in papers and torn-open envelopes. On the other side, a small electric heater was burning in what had once been the old fireplace. A two-burner hotplate stood near it, with a coffee pot and saucepan on top.

But the room was completely empty. Johnny eyed it suspiciously. The chair that belonged to the desk had been turned round, so that anyone sitting in it could have been listening at the door. But on the other hand the store owner could simply have turned it round so that he could sit facing the fire. There was a faint smell of tobacco smoke in the room, but that could have been left there by the store owner too. The room was empty, but there was another door leading out of it into a back alley, as Johnny could see through a small window at the side.

There might have been someone there, or on the other hand there might not. At all events, there was no one there now. Johnny turned to the others, who were still watching him curiously, and shrugged. Then he closed the door again softly and walked back to them.

"Probably just my imagination," he said. "I thought I heard the latch click. Did either of you hear anything?"

Gwen and Gaston shook their heads.

"Oh well," Johnny said. "My mistake. I'm getting jumpy. It's a good job the owner didn't see me nosing into his sitting-room like that, or he really would think that we were acting suspiciously!"

"But Johnny," Gwen said seriously, going back to the subject of the book. "Wherever are we going to get thirty dollars? We've never had that much money."

"Yes, we have to do something quickly," Gaston said. "This man, he is getting suspicious."

"Yes, that's why he took those other books away," Johnny said. "He didn't want to dust them, he wanted to get a good look at them." He thought for a moment, then he turned to Gaston. "Could you copy out the message?" he whispered. "And make a copy of the map?"

Gaston opened the book again and looked at it. "It is too difficult," he said. "I can't read most of the words. It would take me very long, and he would come back." He gestured towards the front of the store.

"Maybe we could tear out the two pages we want," Gwen said, but then she added reluctantly, "but I guess that would be stealing, wouldn't it?"

"Of course it would," Gaston said. "We can't do that."

"Well, if we can't steal the pages, and we haven't got time to copy them out, there's only one thing left," Johnny said. "We'll have to buy the book."

"But thirty dollars!" Gwen said. "We haven't got thirty dollars, so how can we buy it?"

"How much have you got?" Johnny said. "I've got two dollars on me, of my vacation money, and ten cents. And I've got another five dollars vacation money at home. That's seven dollars and ten cents. What have you got?"

Gwen and Johnny got a dollar a week allowance, which their parents paid in advance when they went on holiday, to spend exactly as they liked.

Gwen was adding up. "I've got a dollar and thirty-two cents with me," she said, "and I've still got seven dollars at home. That's eight dollars and thirty-two cents."

"That makes fifteen dollars and forty-two cents altogether," Johnny said. They looked at Gaston, who was going through his pockets.

"I don't know," he said. "I have only twenty-five cents with me, but I could get some more if I went home maybe, to get my bank book."

"How much?" Johnny said.

"How much do you want? I have got fifty dollars in my savings account, nearly."

Johnny hesitated. "Could you get fifteen dollars?" he said. "That would give us just over the thirty dollars we need."

"Oh, Johnny!" Gwen said. "Fifteen dollars!"

Gaston looked serious for a moment and then made up his mind. "No, that is all right," he said. "It is the same as you two are putting in. I will get fifteen dollars. It will be all right as long as my parents don't find out."

"Gee, Gaston, that's great!" Johnny said happily, then paused as the bell on the door of the shop tinkled. There was a faint sound of conversation at the front of the shop for a few moments and then the bell tinkled again as the customer went out.

Johnny went on again. "As soon as we find this

treasure," he said, "you'll be paid back with interest. Your parents won't need to worry then."

"And suppose we don't find the treasure?" Gwen said. "What then? We don't even know that this old book has anything to do with Montcalm."

"Use your imagination!" Johnny said impatiently. "Here's an old French book of sermons over two hundred years old with one sermon in it that talks about treasure. In between the lines of it someone has written a message, and at the end of it there's a map with crosses on it and the words 'Where we have hidden ours.' What else could it be?"

"Yes, but it doesn't say anything about Montcalm," Gwen said, resenting the scorn in her brother's voice. "If it was his, it would have his name in the book somewhere."

"Ah, no, Gwen," Gaston said. "But if it had had Montcalm's name in it, we would never have found it lying in this old trunk here. It would have been put in a museum long ago. It is only because it didn't have Montcalm's name in it maybe, that no one has paid any attention to it. I think no one has probably opened it except us since that message was written there."

"That's right," Johnny said exultantly. "It's just a matter of luck that we were thinking about treasure and that Gaston noticed this sermon about treasure. Otherwise we would never have looked at it either. We weren't even looking in the right place. We were looking at maps."

"Well, all right," Gwen said. "But I just hope you're right. Because if we spend thirty dollars on some old book and it isn't really worth anything at all, we're going to get into a real mess."

Gaston had suddenly begun to look doubtful too. He was turning the book over in his hands and frowning. Then he said, "You are sure we are going to buy this book for thirty dollars, eh?"

"Sure, why not?" Johnny said. "I think the risk's worth taking. We'll leave what money we have as a deposit on it and then we can come back with the rest as soon as we get it."

"But you are sure you can get the money, eh?" Gaston said, still very doubtful. "You are sure we can afford to buy this book?"

"Sure I'm sure," Johnny said. "We can get our part anyway, and I'm willing to risk it." He looked at Gaston with a frown. "What's the matter? D'you think you won't be able to get your fifteen dollars, after all?"

Gaston shook his head. He didn't like the impatience in Johnny's voice. His own answer was slightly angry.

"No, it's not that. But if we put a deposit on the book, it is ours, eh? We have to buy it or we lose our money, but it is ours?"

"Sure. Say, what's the matter?" Johnny said, getting angry because of his disappointment. "Are you trying to chicken out because you might lose your fifteen dollars? We'll pay you back if you lose it. Maybe we can raise all the money ourselves."

"Johnny!" Gwen exclaimed angrily.

Gaston's fists clenched dangerously. "Chicken out?" he said, glaring at Johnny. "I am not the chicken. I show you!"

"Well, okay then," Johnny said, already feeling

ashamed of his outburst. "Let's give him the deposit, get out of here, and go home for the rest of the money. Come on." He turned round and started to the front of the shop.

Gwen started to lift the table leg to release the Mouse, who had been dozing again, this time in a comfortably tight spot between two pieces of furniture, when Gaston stopped her.

"It's okay, I bring him. I just want to fix my shoe." He bent down to retie a loose shoelace, and Gwen walked after Johnny down to the front of the long dark store.

The storekeeper was at the counter, going through the pile of books he had carried away with him. He looked up as they arrived. His smile now seemed almost a sneer.

"We've decided on the book we want," Johnny said. "The only thing is, we don't have thirty dollars on us, so we'd like to leave what money we do have as a deposit while we go home and get the rest. Is that all right?"

"Of course." The man said coldly "Which is the book?" He looked at their hands eagerly.

Johnny looked round for Gaston, and Gwen said, "He's just tying his shoe and bringing the Mouse. He'll be here in a minute." And, just as she said it, Gaston came down the store towards them with the Mouse straining on his leash. He put the book on the counter and the man picked it up quickly and then eyed them all curiously.

"*Is* that one thirty dollars?" Johnny said anxiously.

"Ah . . . yes," the man said, turning it over in his hands. "I should think I could let you have it for that."

He grinned again. "Yes. I'll have it wrapped up for you by the time you return."

Johnny collected all their money together and put it on the counter, and the man counted it out and put it in the cash register.

"We'll be back as soon as we can," Johnny said, looking at the book uneasily. "It's our father's birthday tomorrow, and we want to have the book at home tonight so that we can surprise him in the morning."

"Ah yes, the birthday. Of course." And the man gave one of his most unpleasant dry smiles.

As they went out of the door, Johnny glanced back. The storekeeper had leaned forward on the counter and opened the book. Johnny's heart sank. It was hopeless. If the man went on turning over the pages, he would see the message and the map long before they could get back.

5

The Shadow

They wasted no time arguing about it once they were safely outside the shop. Gaston unlocked his bicycle, which was leaning up against the front of the shop, and said, almost abruptly, "See you back here in half an hour —at the bottom of the steps." Then, before they could do more than say "okay" he was off and pedalling away furiously down the street.

"Hey—," Johnny said, but Gaston was already out of hearing and round the corner. "What's got into him, anyway?" Johnny said disgustedly. "He's acting very strangely all of a sudden. All that fuss about the money inside the shop, and now he goes rushing off some short way home that he knows probably, and leaves us to lug our bicycles all the way up those steps again. One thing, when we come back I'm going to leave them up at the top of the steps, instead of having to carry them all the way down here and up again."

They got on their bicycles and rode to the end of the street where the steps were, with the Mouse running along behind. Then, as they got off and hoisted the bicycles onto their shoulders for the long climb up,

Johnny added, "I don't know. I don't like the way Gaston's acting at all. I think he's up to something. Maybe we shouldn't have told him about the treasure in the first place."

"Oh, Johnny, don't be silly!" Gwen said angrily. "We wouldn't have been able to do a thing without him. We would never have found this shop in the first place, and we certainly would never have found that message in the book if he hadn't been able to read French."

But Johnny remained unconvinced and continued to worry about Gaston's behaviour all the way home and then all the way back again to the top of the steps, where they locked their bicycles and left them leaning against the wall of one of the buildings at the top. He had even begun to suspect that Gaston might be planning to get back before they did, with all the money, to get the book for himself. He certainly had enough money in the bank to do it.

It had taken them longer than they expected to get home, get the money from their cash boxes without attracting their mother's attention, and get back. It was forty minutes by the clock in the post-office tower before they got back, in spite of all Johnny's efforts to hurry.

"He's not here," Johnny said, all his worst fears seeming to have come true as he looked down the steps. They hurried down, with the Mouse at their heels, their feet clattering on the metal stairway, but then, as they turned the corner at the bottom, and looked down the street that Gaston had called *Sous le Fort* to where the shop was, they breathed a sigh of relief. Gaston was pacing towards them, his bicycle already parked outside the shop.

As soon as he saw them, he broke into a run. "Where have you been?" he said urgently. "I am here already since fifteen minutes."

Gwen shot a look at Johnny as if to say "I-told-you-so" about all his suspicions, and then said to Gaston eagerly, "We had a little trouble getting away from our mother. Did you get your money?"

Gaston nodded, put his hand into his pocket and produced three five-dollar bills, which he handed to Johnny. Johnny looked a little shamefaced as he took them.

"That's it," he said. "That makes our thirty dollars. Thanks a lot, Gaston."

Then suddenly Gwen looked quickly back at Gaston. "Why on earth did you put a jacket on, Gaston?" she said. "You must be roasting." And Gaston did indeed look hot. When they had last seen him he had been wearing just an open-necked sport shirt like Johnny, and summer shorts.

"Oh, it was my mother," Gaston mumbled, then added, "let's get back to the shop. We have been gone so long, he could have discovered everything."

"We'll soon know," Johnny said grimly, "by how we're treated when we get inside. If he's found the map and the message he certainly isn't going to let us have the book."

But when they got into the shop they got a pleasant surprise. The shopkeeper stood up from behind the counter and took down a carefully gift-wrapped package from the shelf behind him. "Ah, the book collectors!" he said, looking from one to the other of them with his yellow teeth showing. "So you did come back. Good. I have it already wrapped for you."

Johnny pulled the money from his pocket and put it on the counter, looking at the package suspiciously. Certainly the man didn't seem to suspect anything, but how could they be sure he was giving them the right book in this package? Maybe he hadn't found anything yet, but was keeping back the book they really wanted, to examine it more closely after they were gone. Yet they couldn't tear the gift-wrapping off right away to check, or he would realize that there was something very special about the book they wanted, and in that case he would probably refuse to let them have it anyway.

Johnny looked at Gwen and Gaston in bewilderment as these thoughts flashed through his mind. He couldn't tell whether they realized the problem too, or not. Gwen was watching the man count out the money and Gaston was rummaging in his pockets looking for something.

"I think I dropped my handkerchief at the back of the store," Gaston said. "I'll go and see."

The man looked up briefly from checking the money and nodded. "This all seems to be correct," he said. "Twenty-six dollars and thirty-three cents, and the three dollars and sixty-seven cents that you gave me before. Thirty dollars." He rang it up on the cash register and pushed the book towards them across the counter. "There you are," he said. "And many happy returns of the day to your father. I'm sure he'll be delighted."

Johnny hesitated for one moment more as the man stared at him, and then picked up the package. There wasn't anything they could do about it now, except hope that all their suspicions had been groundless. Maybe it was the right book after all.

Gaston came back from the rear of the store, wiping his nose vigorously. "I found it," he said.

Johnny put the book under his arm and turned for the door. "Thank you," he said. He could hardly wait to get outside so that they could open it.

As soon as they were outside Johnny said, "Come on, let's get away from the front of the shop and have a look at it. I've got a feeling that this is all too easy. That guy may have switched books on us."

Gaston pushed his bicycle out into the street and they hurried along towards the foot of the steps. As they went, Johnny began to tear the gift-wrapping off the book. He looked at the title on the back quickly. "Well, *whadda ya know?*" he said, with an enormous grin. "It's okay! It's the right book! *Sermons de Monseigneur Philippe de Brébeuf!* Good old Brébeuf!" He opened it excitedly as they reached the bottom of the steps, while Gaston watched him with a sudden broad grin. Johnny riffled through the pages quickly, hunting for the place, and then began to look puzzled.

"That's funny," he said. "I can't find it. What page was it?"

He handed the book to Gaston, who was still grinning broadly, and Gaston looked at it. Then his grin faded. "This is not the right book," he said. "He does suspect something. He has kept the one we wanted."

"But it's the right title!" Johnny said in amazement.

"Yes, but this is volume two. We wanted volume one. He knows that we are on to something. Let's get out of here before he decides to follow us." He handed the book

back to Johnny and began to pick up his bicycle, ready
for the climb up the steps.

"What! And leave him behind with the map and
message?" Johnny said indignantly. "He's cheated us.
We've got to go right back and demand the book we
paid for. He's cheated us out of thirty dollars, and he's
got the map and message!"

"Oh dear!" Gwen wailed. "I just knew something
terrible would happen. We never should have let him
have the money before we'd had a chance to look at
the book."

"Never mind about that now!" Johnny said. "Let's
go back there and threaten him that we'll tell the police."

"That is not necessary," Gaston said, grabbing
Johnny's arm. "Come with me to the top of the steps,
away from here, and I will tell you why."

"Not necessary!" Johnny said. "Are you crazy? He's
got the map and the message!"

"He has not got the map, or the message," Gaston
said, looking round anxiously. "I have got them."

"You've got them!" Johnny said in amazement.
"Where? How?"

"In my inside pocket," Gaston said, opening his jacket
to show them the two folded, yellow pages sticking out
of the lining of the coat. "I cut them out with my knife
the first time we were in the shop and hid them, when I
stayed behind to tie up my shoe."

"You did!" Johnny said, reaching over and slapping
Gaston on the shoulder. "Oh boy! And that guy thinks
that he's tricked us!"

Gwen clapped her hands. "Then that's why you

came back wearing your jacket—so that you could smuggle them out?"

"Yes, he would have seen them if I had tried to hide them in my shirt. It is too thin. So I had to hide them in the store first, to make sure he didn't find them in the book while we were away."

"Oh boy, what a brain!" Johnny said admiringly. "Gaston, I'll take back everything I ever said about you. I thought you were acting suspiciously, and you sure were!"

"And that's why you wanted to be so sure that we would be able to buy the book?" Gwen said. "And why you said you had to go to the back of the store to look for your handkerchief just now?"

"I had to be sure we could buy the book," Gaston said apologetically. "Otherwise it would have been like stealing to take the pages."

"Don't apologize, man!" Johnny said gleefully. "You deserve a medal. Boy, wait until that guy goes through that book really carefully and finds that the two pages he's looking for have been cut out!"

"That's it," Gaston said. "It may not take him so long to find out that he has been tricked. He had all that time when we were away to go through the book, and he has probably started looking again now. That's why I want to get away from here before he does find out something. Let us go up the top of the steps, anyway."

They looked back at the shop uneasily. It was quite true. As soon as the shopkeeper found out that instead of tricking them, he had been tricked himself, he would try to track them down. Best to get away now, before he had the chance.

There were a couple of people walking in the street and one man standing looking in the antique-shop window, who turned round as they were looking at him and began to walk slowly down the street in their direction. But there was no sign of the storekeeper.

Gaston hoisted his bicycle up onto his shoulder and began climbing. "We can have a look at the things when we get to the top," he said.

"There's one thing I don't understand," Johnny said as they climbed, "and that's how he caught on to us in the first place. He seemed to suspect we were on to something from the very first moment when we went into the shop. And then how did he know that there was anything special in that book that we wanted? He couldn't have heard us whispering at the back of the shop when he was in the front all the time." And then he had a sudden thought. "Unless he has the whole place wired for microphones."

But then, at once, he shook his head. "No, that's too fantastic. Why would anyone have an old shop like that wired for microphones?"

"Unless it's something to do with what Gaston's father told him," Gwen said. "About the man being a receiver of stolen goods."

"That wouldn't have anything to do with it," Johnny said impatiently. "What would microphones have to do with that?"

"There was someone in the room at the back after all, perhaps," Gaston said, grunting under the weight of his bicycle. "Someone was listening perhaps, eh? But who?"

A faint warning bell began to ring at the back of Johnny's brain. Perhaps there had been someone there.

That had to be it. Someone who had heard just enough to know what they were looking for, and who had noticed their excitement when they found the book. Someone who had slipped out of the back room just before he had opened the door and looked in, and who maybe had gone round to the front of the store to warn the shopkeeper.

Suddenly the memory of another faint ringing chimed in with that of the warning bell: the tinkle of the bell of the shop! That was it! That customer they had heard come in while they were still arguing at the back of the shop, a customer who had stayed only a few moments and then left again—that could be him, coming in to warn his partner not to sell the book they wanted and then slipping out again, perhaps back round to the rear of the store to hear what else they might say.

How much had he heard—if it was a man? Obviously he hadn't seen Gaston cutting and hiding the all-important pages, and obviously he hadn't heard enough to be able to tell his partner exactly where to look in the book, or what to look for, or else the storekeeper would have discovered before they returned that the pages he was looking for had been cut out. He obviously hadn't suspected that at all.

But how much had the man heard? And, above all, who was he? Had it just been bad luck that he had been in that back room when they came in, or was it more than bad luck?

Again that alarm bell began ringing, more loudly this time, but this time he could find no answer. How could there be anything more? How could the shopkeeper have known anything about them before they had even set foot in the store? It was impossible. It was just bad luck. And only Gaston's quick-wittedness had saved them from the consequences.

As they got to the top of the steps, they paused for a moment and looked down, Gaston panting from the climb and the weight of his bicycle. The only person on the stairs was the man they had seen looking in the antique-shop window, about a third of the way up and climbing slowly. The shopkeeper hadn't discovered anything yet anyway, and if he came out now, he wouldn't know which way they had gone.

Gwen and Johnny unlocked their bicycles at the spot where they had left them at the top of the steps, and then all three of them moved farther round the corner from the steps, where they would be out of sight from the street below. Gaston pulled the two sheets of paper out of his pocket. Gwen and Johnny crowded nearer to get a look at the writing.

"What does it say, Gaston?" Gwen said. "Can you read it at all now in the daylight?"

"Well, the map is all right. I can read that: 'Isle of Sorcerers,' then 'Where we have hidden ours,' and the crosses. But the message is very difficult. I can see some of the words. It says 'Isle of Sorcerers' again, and something about saying your prayers. Then 'full moon' and something about a wheel and a serpent, and then some words about where dead men go. It is very difficult. The writing is faint, and the spelling seems to be old-fashioned."

"Holy Moses," Gwen said. "It sounds bad enough anyway! Sorcerers, serpents, and dead men! No wonder we've got to say our prayers!"

"Where is this Isle of Sorcerers, anyway?" Johnny said. "Have you ever heard of it, Gaston?"

Gaston shook his head. "I never heard of any island called that around here."

"Well, I've got a magnifying glass at home," Johnny said. "We should be able to make out the writing more easily with that. Let's go and get it."

Suddenly Gwen reached across and squeezed Johnny's arm, nodding vigorously in the direction of the steps behind them. "Well, I think the whole thing's a lot of nonsense," she said. "I vote that we just forget about it."

Johnny and Gaston looked puzzled, and then followed the direction of her glance. The sun was shining directly through the steep stairway they had just climbed, throwing bright sunlight through the gap it made between the buildings at the top. They were around the corner from the stairway now, standing in the shade of the buildings, so that they could no longer actually see the steps. But there on the ground in front of them as they turned round was the shadow of a man, standing at the top of the steps, pressed up against the wall. He was only about five yards from them, completely out of sight round the corner of the building. If it hadn't been for his shadow, they would never have known he was there. And he was close enough to have overheard every word they had said. . . .

6

A Riddle in Rhyme

They looked at each other for a moment in silence, and then back at the shadow. There was no doubt that the man was standing there listening to them, and Johnny suddenly remembered that the man they had seen looking in the antique-shop window and climbing the steps behind them had never come out from the top of the steps. He might have gone down again, or on the other hand. . . . Was this the man from the back room, the storekeeper's unknown partner? If so, he knew now that they had got what they wanted, after all.

Gaston had taken a pencil out of his pocket and scribbled something on the back of one of the pages from the book. He handed it over to Johnny now, and he and Gwen looked at it. "Keep talking, and ride off," it said. They looked at Gaston and nodded, and then he pointed down the hill, past the opening at the top of the stairway where the man was standing. It was the direction opposite to the one they ought to take to get home, but it was downhill and they would be away before the man even realized what was happening. That way too, they might

get a glimpse of him as they rode past and see exactly who it was that was on their trail.

"Well, maybe Gwen's right," Johnny drawled loudly, as they all climbed into their saddles. "Maybe they never have lived around here." He winked at the others. "Let's have another look at that road map again. Now!"

As he said this last word, he waved the other two on and they all started pedalling together, pushing off with one foot and heading past the top of the stairway before the man behind the wall had a chance to realize what they were doing. They twisted their heads and tried to get a look at him as they shot past, but the man threw his hand up to cover his face as soon as he saw them. All they got was a glance at him: average size, no hat, a light brown suit and brown shoes. Then they were past him, bending over their handlebars and pedalling furiously to get out of his range before he could attempt to stop them. It was the man who had followed them up the steps all right: they recognized the clothes; but as to who he was they had no further clue.

As they turned the corner at the foot of the hill Gaston, who was leading, pulled into the curb quickly and stopped. The others put on their brakes and stopped beside him.

"What are you stopping for?" Johnny asked urgently. "If he's following us he won't be far behind. I know it's the same guy we saw looking into the store window, but who he is beats me. I wish I'd taken a proper look at him when we had the chance."

"I think that I have seen him somewhere around the city," Gaston said. "But I don't know. There's something about him." He frowned in concentration, then shook his head hopelessly and pulled out the two sheets of paper from his pocket. He handed one of them over to Johnny.

"We had better split up," he said. "You take the map, and I will take the message and try to work on it at home. Even if he tries, he can't follow both of us. This way we'll probably lose him altogether. I will come to your house tonight, about seven o'clock, after supper."

Johnny took the map and glanced behind him nervously. "Right," he said. "And now let's get out of here."

The others needed no urging. In a moment they were heading on down the main street at full speed, and soon Gaston took a side street which would take him a different way home. Once more, as they parted, Johnny looked back, then they were in a stream of traffic, heading for home. There was no further sign of the man, only more traffic behind them, and in front of them, and on all sides, and Johnny breathed a sigh of relief. They seemed to have thrown him off the track for good.

However, it was only when Gaston arrived at their house that night, a little after seven, that they finally felt completely safe, and even then Gwen still had her doubts. Her first words, after they had introduced Gaston to their parents and taken him out into the garden, were very serious.

"You know," she said doubtfully, "I've been thinking. Maybe we should tell Mummy and Daddy. If someone really is after us, this isn't a game any more. And now that we've got proof of the treasure, they'll listen to us."

Gaston shook his head. "No good," he said. "They will still think you are fooling, like my father. I showed him the message and he laughed. He thought it was a game I was playing with someone."

"You showed him the message?" Johnny said. "Why?"

"I had to ask him to help me translate it," Gaston said. "It was too difficult for me. Many of the words are in old French, and it is written in some kind of code."

"A code?" Gwen said. "What kind of code? Did he help you?"

"*Oui.* He helped me, but he wouldn't believe it was serious. He thought it was just some game I had got out of a book. Every time I tried to tell him, he just mocked at me. It is no good with adults. They do not believe some things."

"No imagination," Johnny agreed, shaking his head. It was his usual complaint. "No, we'll have to go this alone. They'll never believe us. Anyway, if we tell them we've paid thirty dollars for some old book of sermons they'll blow their tops."

"But what about the translation?" Gwen said. "Did you bring it with you?"

"Yes, here it is, and here is the original message from the book," Gaston said, pulling the two pieces of paper from his pocket, one old and yellow, the other white and new.

Johnny pulled the map out of his pocket. "Right, let's get cracking," he said.

Just then Mrs Matthews came out into the garden carrying a tray with three fresh lemonades on it. As soon as they saw her they stopped talking, and Gaston got up to help her with the tray.

"Now what are you three plotting?" she said, looking from one to the other of them. "Thank you, Gaston."

"We're looking for that buried treasure of Mont-calm's, Mom," Johnny said, with a look at Gaston.

Mrs Matthews laughed. "Oh well, if you need any help spending it when you find it," she said, "just let me know." She went back into the house.

"You see," Johnny said. "They really don't believe anything. They think that buried treasure is just something you read about in books."

They began sipping their drinks and then spread the papers out on their knees.

"Okay, Gaston, let's have it," Johnny said.

Gaston looked at the two pieces of paper thought-fully. "Well," he said, "the original message was written as a kind of poem, and when my father translated it," Gaston began to smile, "he insisted on doing the same kind of poem in English too. That's why I was late. I told him just to write it the way it was, but he likes puzzles and things and he was enjoying himself trying to make it rhyme in English. It doesn't come out too good as poetry, I think," he said apologetically. "I told him to leave it." He handed the piece of paper over to Johnny, who read it aloud:

> *Backwards you must say your prayers,*
> *In the Isle of Sorcerers,*
> *Where the worshippers all kneel,*
> *To a Lady with a Wheel.*
> *Then, when summer moons are full,*
> *You will see a serpent coil.*
> *Grasp its head, and come below,*
> *Where none but the dead should go.*

"Holy crow!" Johnny added. "What does *that* mean?" He read it out loud again.

"I don't know what it means, and I'm not sure I want to," Gwen said. "Go where none but dead men should go! Not me! Not if I can help it!"

"Yes, it is a puzzle okay, eh?" Gaston said. "Maybe the map will help solve it. Maybe we can make them fit together."

"Well, that's another funny thing," Johnny said. "We've been looking at the map, and it doesn't really tell you anything at all. It's not like any treasure map I've ever seen in books or anything. They always have directions on them—how many paces from this tree to that tree, and so on. But this one is just a plain map of an island, with that name Isle of Sorcerers written over it, and then those other words about where we have buried ours, and then there are six crosses in different places around the coast. And that's all. There's no other writing or anything. I don't know what that's supposed to mean at all."

They sat and puzzled over it, and then Gwen said, "Maybe it's got some other writing on it in invisible ink. They do have sometimes, when people want to hide something. They write on them in lemon juice and things and then you have to heat the paper over a fire or a candle to make the writing show up."

Johnny frowned at the map. "That's an idea," he said. "There's certainly got to be something more than this." He got up. "I'll go and get a candle. And I'll get some paper and we can make a tracing of the map as well, in case we manage to set fire to it. We really would be sunk then."

He went into the house and came back in a few minutes with a short piece of candle and a book of matches in one hand and a notebook and pencil in the other.

"Gaston, you hold the map out flat," he said, "and I'll hold the candle under it and make sure it doesn't catch fire. You look at the top of it, Gwen, and tell us if anything starts appearing."

They did just as he said, and Johnny knelt down on the grass, lit the candle, and held it underneath the stretched sheet of paper at a safe distance. Gwen peered at the paper, but nothing happened. Seconds passed and Johnny said, "Isn't there anything there yet? The underneath of the paper is getting all black with the candle smoke."

Gwen shook her head, then looked again more closely. "Now there's something," she said. "But it's not words. The paper's starting to go brown in the middle. Oh, I think it's scorching! Take the candle away! Quick!"

But Johnny already had. He blew the flame out and threw the stub of candle to one side, where it was promptly seized and eaten with great relish by the Mouse, who had come out from the house and had been watching the whole performance with considerable interest.

They looked at the paper, and the Mouse looked at it too, thinking that it might prove a tasty dessert to follow his little snack. In the middle of the map was a faint brown scorch mark and on the other side a large black circle of candle smoke.

"I knew we should have copied it before we started

experimenting," Johnny said. "I'd better do it now, before something else happens."

He put the map under the top page of his notebook and traced the lines and crosses carefully through the paper, putting everything in the exact place where it was on the original map, including the writing. Then he took the old map out again.

"Well, at least we've got a copy," he said. "But I don't see how there can be any invisible writing on it anyway. It would have shown up before now. There must be something else."

They sat staring at the map again in silence. Then Gwen said, "Those Xs . . . an X is generally the way people mark a treasure on a map, isn't it, Johnny? Does that mean that this treasure is divided into six different places?"

"I don't know," he said. "It might mean that, but we don't even know where the island is yet. That's the first thing we've got to find out, before we can do anything else. You said you've never heard of any island with that name around here, didn't you, Gaston?"

"That's right. But there are very many islands. It could be one I never heard of."

"You know, this may be something that Dad can help us with," Johnny said. "He's down here studying all about Quebec history and places for that history book he's supposed to write. Couldn't he find out where it is from one of his old reference books?"

"Come on, then," Gwen said, already running up the garden. "Let's go ask him."

They raced up behind her and followed her into the living-room.

"Dad!" Gwen burst out.

"Dad!" Johnny said.

"Where's the Isle of Sorcerers?" they both panted together.

"*Oui*, Mr Matthews," Gaston added. "*L'Île des Sorcières?*"

Their father looked up from his book, then across at his wife in surprise. "The Isle of Sorcerers?" he said. "Now how would you know about the Isle of Sorcerers? That's a spot with a pretty spooky reputation."

"Well, where is it, Dad? And what's wrong with it?" Johnny said.

Mr Matthews stood up and took a book off the shelf above his chair. "One question at a time," he said, flipping through the pages. "Ah, here it is. The Isle of Sorcerers . . ." He put the book down again on his knee for a moment and looked at them. "But, there's one thing I can tell you right away," he said with a smile. "If you've got any ideas about Montcalm burying his treasure there, you can forget them. It's impossible."

Johnny, Gwen, and Gaston stared at him blankly, their hearts sinking. What now?

7

Fear in the Night

Mr Matthews's smile broadened as he saw their faces drop. "Guessed right, did I?" he said. "Well, now then, here's what the book has to say about the Isle of Sorcerers." He began to read:

"This island was originally called The Isle of Bacchus, after the Roman god of wine, because of the many wild vines found there. But later, strange lights were seen on the island by the inhabitants, will o' the wisps, which led those poor people who followed them to their deaths in the marshes. The people therefore said that these lights were the work of evil spirits, sorcerers or ghosts, haunting the earth to capture souls for the devil. And the island was renamed the Isle of Sorcerers and became a place of evil reputation."

Mr Matthews looked up at them over the top of the book. "Now, what would you want with a place like that?" he said.

They were silent for a moment, looking at each other. Then Johnny said, "Yes, but where is it, Dad?"

"Well, it doesn't have quite as bad a reputation now," his father said, smiling. "I've been meaning to take you there for an outing before too long. It's called the Island of Orleans now."

"*L'Île d'Orléans*!" Gaston exclaimed excitedly. "That's just down the river, outside Quebec."

"That's right," Mr Matthews said. "About six miles away."

"But what's this about Montcalm, Dad?" Johnny said, trying to seem unconcerned. "Why couldn't he have buried his treasure there?"

"Because if General Montcalm had had a treasure, which I've already told you is very uncertain, and if he had wanted to bury it somewhere, he would hardly have taken it right into the middle of the British camp."

"Ah, *oui*," Gaston said glumly. "That's right. General Wolfe landed on the *Île d'Orléans* and made it his headquarters before he attacked Quebec City. All the inhabitants went away before the British troops came. There was a big panic."

Mrs Matthews laughed out loud at their three glum faces. "Never mind," she said. "Don't take it so badly. Maybe you've discovered someone else's treasure by mistake. Now go and bring those lemonade glasses in from the garden. It'll soon be time for bed."

Johnny went back out of the house, kicking the ground with his toes thoughtfully, followed by Gwen and Gaston. Gwen was the first to speak, when they were out of hearing of the house.

"I told you, Johnny," she said. "I told you in the shop that the book probably had nothing to do with Montcalm, and you wouldn't listen. Well, now we've spent thirty dollars on an old book of sermons and it'll be Daddy's birthday in a few days and when we can't buy him a present Mummy'll want to know what we did with all our pocket money! What a mess!"

"Oh, shut up!" Johnny said irritably. "I'm trying to think." He stood staring at the ground with a frown of concentration. "You really think General Montcalm wouldn't have hidden his treasure on the Island of Orleans, eh Gaston?" he said finally.

"No. It is impossible," Gaston said. "But don't forget, we only thought this was a map and a message for Montcalm's treasure because we were already looking for Montcalm's treasure. It didn't say anything about Montcalm in the book anyway. Maybe your mother is right. Maybe we have found somebody else's treasure by mistake."

"That's right," Gwen said, brightening. "She was only joking, but we do still have the map and the message. Even if they're not the clues to Montcalm's treasure, they must have been left by someone."

"Sure," Johnny said, as they all gradually recovered their spirits. "All this means is that we don't know whose treasure we're on to. And at least we know now that it's hidden on the Island of Orleans. That's something. And if it's only six miles away we can easily get there on our bicycles."

"Yes," Gaston said. "But it is not very much help, because the island is so big. It is about forty miles round and we could search forever with only those crosses to guide us. We have to know more than that."

"Well, what about the message?" Gwen said. "We haven't worked that out yet. That must give us directions about where to look."

They sat down and looked at it again. "Let's go over it from the beginning," Johnny said. "First of all, the first line: *Backwards you must say your prayers*. What does that mean? What prayers?"

"There's the one we used to say when we were little," Gwen said.

Now I lay me down to sleep,
I pray the Lord my soul to keep.
What's that backwards?"

Johnny wrote it down in his notebook and then read it out to them backwards:

Keep to soul my Lord the pray I,
Sleep to down me lay I now.
That doesn't make any kind of sense. Maybe it's in code, too."

"Don't forget," Gaston said. "The message was in French, so it will be a prayer in French, too."

"That's right," Johnny said. "Well, what's the most famous prayer in French? What prayer does every French Canadian know? The Lord's Prayer?"

"*Le Pater*, we call it," Gaston said. "Yes, or maybe the *Ave Maria* is even more famous with Catholics. It goes *Ave Maria, pleine de grâce* . . . Hail Mary, full of grace. . . ."

"Can you write it down, Gaston?" Gwen said. "Then we can see what it looks like backwards. It may not be in code."

Gaston took the notebook and pencil and wrote out the prayer, and then read it over backwards. But it didn't seem to make any sense at all. Johnny sat down in his garden chair again and groaned.

"This is hopeless," he said. "We don't even know if

this really is the right prayer. And even if it is, it must be in code, and we have no way of knowing what the code is!"

Gwen looked up at Gaston. "You said your father liked solving puzzles and things," she said. "Maybe he could try writing those two prayers backwards for us, to see if they mean anything. D'you think he would?"

Gaston's face lit up. "*Eh, voilà*," he said. "You have one good brain, little Gwen. My father is just crazy about things like that. If it is a code, he will love to solve it. I will ask him tonight, when I go home."

Gwen was pleased with the compliment and made a face at her brother, who was always telling her how stupid she was. But for once he didn't try to take a swipe at her.

"Okay," he said, getting up. "We'll have to wait and see what happens. D'you think he'll be able to tell us by tomorrow morning?"

"I dunno, but I will ask him tonight," Gaston said, "and he will tell me in the morning if he has found anything. I will go home right now and see him."

"I guess we'd better go in, too," Johnny said, picking up the tray of empty lemonade glasses. "It's getting kind of late, and there's nothing more we can do until we get that information. There's one thing—if that crook at the shop or that other guy who followed us do have this message, they'll be having just as much trouble as we are finding out what it means."

They walked into the house. "How could they have it?" Gwen said. "They'd obviously never looked at that book before we found it. And Gaston had cut the pages out before they got a chance to see it."

"I guess that's right," Johnny said, as he put the glasses down in the kitchen and then walked with Gaston to the door. "We've got them licked this time. They don't even know where we are."

It was not long before he found out how wrong he was.

After Gaston had left, Johnny and Gwen went into the kitchen for their regular evening snack of milk and cookies and then went upstairs to bed, Johnny carefully carrying the two pages from the old book of sermons and his notebook. The last thing he did, after he had put on his pyjamas and brushed his teeth, was to arrange the pages carefully on his bedside table, where he could lean on his elbow and look at them.

After a while, he lay back, thinking about the message. It was a strange one all right, but then, from what his father had told them, the Isle of Sorcerers was a strange place too. *Strange lights . . . which led those poor people who followed them to their deaths in the marshes. . . . ghosts, haunting the earth to capture souls for the devil.* It certainly didn't have a very healthy reputation. But that would make it an ideal place to hide a treasure. Not many people would come snooping around a place like that.

But what about the six crosses? Was the treasure really divided into six places, as Gwen had suggested, and was their clue to it really hidden in the Lord's Prayer, or some other prayer, when it was said backwards? Ah well, maybe Gaston's father would be able to tell them that . . . in the morning. And with happy thoughts of the morning, Johnny fell asleep.

It must have been hours later when he suddenly woke

up. He had been dreaming of the Mouse squeezing himself into a big wooden trunk full of treasure, and then rolling around happily in a pile of diamonds and rubies and gold coins, barking the Lord's Prayer backwards. But had he really heard a dog barking? He listened carefully, but the house was completely still. His parents must have gone to bed long ago. The moonlight was streaming through a gap in his window curtains, making a long white mark over the ceiling and down one of the walls.

No. Everything was quiet. He must have been imagining things. Then, with a little sigh, he rolled over and went to sleep again.

How much later was it when he was suddenly awake again, his skin prickling with fright? What was it this time? What had he heard? A click of a door handle and the creak of a door opening? Perhaps someone was going to the bathroom, Gwen or one of his parents? But then why did he hear no footsteps?

No, suddenly he had the feeling that someone was in the room with him.

He lay with his back to the bedroom door, facing the moonlight on the wall. The moonlight had moved round a bit now, showing that he had been asleep for some time again. Whoever was there was on the other side of him, looking at him. He was paralysed with fright, afraid to turn round.

Was it just one of those frights that you get sometimes, when you wake up suddenly and imagine that there is someone or something evil in the room with you? Was he just imagining things? Or was there really someone there? If he kept absolutely still and pretended

to be asleep, perhaps they would go away again. Then, as he became wider awake, he began to pull himself together. There was nothing to be afraid of. His father and mother were in the house, just a couple of rooms away.

There was another slight noise, and he suddenly sat up in bed and turned round, his heart thumping—just in time to see a white hand pulling away from his bed. He gave a yell, half of fright and half of defiance, and caught a sudden glimpse of a dark shape. Then something soft and heavy was thrown over his head, preventing him from seeing anything, and he was pushed back down on the bed. He heard his door open and the sound of running feet on the stairs and sat up again, struggling to untangle himself from whatever it was over his head, yelling at the top of his voice.

All at once he had the blanket off his head—it was the spare blanket from the foot of his own bed!—and was out of bed and on his feet, ready to follow. Before he could reach the top of the stairs, he was grabbed from behind by a strong pair of hands.

"What on earth's going on?" his father said sleepily, as he grabbed him. "What's all the shouting about?"

"There was someone in my room," Johnny blurted. "He ran down the stairs."

His father turned and walked down the stairs, turning on the lights as he went, and Johnny's mother came and held him back as he tried to follow. But, after a few moments, when his father had made a quick tour of the downstairs, trying the doors and windows, and had even looked out into the garden, he came back shaking his head.

"There's no one there," he said, "and nothing seems to have been disturbed. I think you must have been having a nightmare, my boy, and got tangled up in your own blanket."

And try as he might, he couldn't convince them that there had been anyone there.

His mother took him back into his room, folded up the spare blanket again, and then sat on the side of the bed for a while until she was sure he had calmed down. Then she said good night again and went out, closing the door behind her softly.

There *had* been someone there! He knew that he hadn't just been having a nightmare. He had seen that hand. And the blanket had been thrown on him as soon as he sat up.

Suddenly he looked at his bedside table. The map and the message were gone!

He leaned over the side of the bed to see if by any chance they had fallen on the floor, but they were gone all right. So that was it! The man must have managed to follow them, after all, maybe in a taxi. And he had known that it would be too dangerous to try to take the papers from them in the street, with all kinds of people around. He had just wanted to find out where they lived, so that he could break in during the night and hunt around for the papers without any fuss. And now he had them, he and his accomplice, the storekeeper. Whoever the second man was, they now knew for sure that the two of them were after the treasure too, and that they would probably stop at nothing to get to it before he and Gwen and Gaston did.

8

Devil Worship

The first thing Johnny did when he went downstairs the next morning was look round the house for some clue as to how the burglar had got in without waking anybody. He found it in the front room. The only windows in the house without screens were the ones that looked out onto the front porch, and these opened outwards on hinges. Because they had no screens, they had been kept latched, and they were latched now. But it was clear that one of them had been used the night before, and that whoever had used it had relatched it behind him. On the centre cushion of the chesterfield, right where anyone would have had to step on it if he had come in through the window, was the heavy and rather dirty impression of a foot. It wasn't the kind of thing his father would have noticed in the middle of the night, but Johnny was looking for it. He unlatched the window and looked at it. There were some fresh, bright scratches on the paint around the latch which told the same story. It had been opened from outside.

The thief could have come in that way, and then let himself out quietly through the front door as he ran off with the map and the message. Nothing else seemed to have been disturbed.

Johnny smoothed out the cushion, brushing off the small amount of loose dirt, and relatched the window before going in to breakfast. There was no point in getting his parents excited about it now. If he did convince them that someone had broken into the house, they would simply call in the police, and that would be the end of the treasure as far as he and Gwen and Gaston were concerned.

"We started this thing and we want to finish it," he said to Gwen, when they were alone at the breakfast table. "Why should we let anyone else in on it now, especially the police, when we're getting so close? We can tell them about it when we've actually found the treasure."

"If these crooks don't get to it first," Gwen said ominously, poking at her cereal. "Besides, if they've stolen the map and the message, how are we going to—"

"Don't forget we still have the copy of the map that I made last night," Johnny said, interrupting her, "and the translation of the message that Gaston's father made. They were both in my notebook. They didn't get those. And they'll have just as much trouble understanding that message as we're having."

"If Gaston's father hasn't understood it already," Gwen said eagerly. "If he's solved that thing about saying your prayers backwards, we may still beat them to it."

"Right!" Johnny said. "So let's get over to Gaston's right away to see if he's got anything to tell us."

Right after breakfast they got out their bicycles and

set off, with the Mouse riding in his usual place in the basket in front of Gwen. But when they arrived at Gaston's house it was to find a long-faced friend awaiting them.

"What's wrong, Gaston?" Gwen said, as soon as she saw how gloomy he looked. "Couldn't your father solve the code?"

"It is not that," Gaston said. "There is not any code."

"No code!" Johnny echoed. "But did he try the Lord's Prayer backwards, or that other prayer? Or maybe there was some other prayer that he could have tried."

"No, that is not it," Gaston said wearily. "I gave my father the paper with the words of the *Ave Maria* written on it backwards, to try that one first, and asked him if he could find the message in it, as if it was some game. At first he didn't know what it was and began to look at it to solve it. But then he looked surprised and said that what I had given him was the *Ave Maria* written backwards. I said I knew that it was, but that there was some message supposed to be hidden in it and could he find it?—or maybe in the *Pater* written backwards. But he said that it was forbidden to write these prayers backwards or say them backwards. He told me that that was how some people in olden times used to worship the Devil. It was called the Black Mass when they did that, and when they said these prayers backwards the Devil would come to them out of the ground."

Johnny and Gwen stared at him in astonishment, and then sat down on either side of him on the front steps.

"You mean that what the message is saying is that we actually have to *say* our prayers backwards on the island," Johnny said, "and then the Devil will appear or something!"

"The Isle of Sorcerers!" Gwen said, breathlessly. "Then it's true! You remember what Daddy told us about how the place used to be haunted by evil spirits who were sent there to trap souls for the Devil? This must all be connected with it."

"I don't believe it," Johnny said. "There must be some other explanation. Let's see, how does the rest of that rhyme go? *Backwards you must say your prayers, In the Isle of Sorcerers*—at least we know what the last part means: that's the Island of Orleans. Then, *Where the worshippers all kneel, To a Lady with a Wheel.* Now, what on earth does that mean?"

"I told you what it means," Gaston said. "It means we have to worship the Devil and then he comes to help us and takes us all to Hell."

"Oh, that's crazy," Johnny said. "You don't really believe in the Devil and Hell and all that stuff, do you? That's just a story. They don't really exist."

"Of course they exist," Gaston said. "It is you who are the crazy one if you don't think so. How could Our Lord go down into Hell as the Bible says if it was not so? And He was tempted three times by the Devil in the wilderness."

"Well," Gwen said hesitantly. "But that doesn't really mean that the Devil is a real person, does it? Or that Hell is a real place? I mean, it could just be a way of describing things. Like when you feel tempted to do something wrong, you could say it was the Devil tempting you to do it, although really it was just something inside of you wanting to be wicked."

"Why should it not be the Devil who was inside you, then?" Gaston said. "You think he cannot go where he pleases, even inside people?"

"Look, this is crazy," Johnny said, trying to restore peace. "This hasn't got anything to do with the Bible or what you believe. This is just a clue about how to find some buried treasure. It simply says we have to say our prayers backwards in the Island of Orleans, in some particular place, and then something will happen. How does it go? *Then, when summer moons are full, You will see a serpent coil.* We'll see a serpent coil? Gosh, I don't know how it works but it certainly hasn't got anything to do with the Devil and all that stuff."

"Then why do you have to say your prayers backwards, then, if that is so?" Gaston said fiercely. "That is the Devil, that serpent. That is how he came to Adam and Eve in the Garden of Eden—disguised as a serpent."

"Oh, come on," Johnny said in disgust. "The Garden of Eden! For Pete's sake!"

Gaston bridled. "Well, then, you tell me what else could happen if you say your prayers backwards. You tell me that. It is evil and I will not do it, even for a buried treasure."

"Well, I will," Johnny said. "I'd say the whole Bible backwards if I had to, to help me find this treasure. That's just superstition."

"You are sinful, if you say that," Gaston said angrily, standing up. "You are not even a Christian if you would do that!"

"Who's not a Christian?" Johnny said, getting up and facing him. "Just because you go to the Catholic church, you think you're the only Christian?"

"You would worship the Devil for money!" Gaston snapped.

"Money's got nothing to do with religion, stupid!" Johnny snapped back.

"So? Stupid?" Gaston said, pushing him. "Atheist!"

Johnny grabbed him, they tripped each other and in a moment they were rolling on the sidewalk outside the house wrestling with each other just as they had outside the museum the day they had met. The Mouse began to bark excitedly again, too, and jump around them. It seemed that they were back right where they had started.

"Oh dear! Stop it, the two of you!" Gwen said, pulling at them and trying to separate them. "Look out, here's someone coming!"

A young priest had been walking along the other side of the street in his swinging black robes, but he stopped when he saw them begin to fight. Now he started across the road. He stood over them for a moment, and then leaned down and pulled them apart.

"Now, now, peace, my young friends. Come, come, what is all this about?"

They were both silent for a moment, and then Gaston broke into a torrent of French, explaining. The priest listened until he had finished and then led them both by the arm over to the steps and sat down between them. Gwen stood anxiously on one leg by their side.

The priest now asked Johnny for his version of the fight and Johnny told him, but only about the argument about the Devil and Hell, carefully omitting any mention of the treasure. The priest listened, and then nodded his head.

"I see," he said, smiling faintly. "And might I ask how this curious argument arose? It isn't often that I find young men of your age so violently interested in matters of religion."

The two boys looked at each other in silence for a moment. Neither of them had mentioned the treasure. Gwen broke in.

"We were reading a story," she said. "And in this story there was a secret message about how to find some lost treasure. It said that you had to say your prayers backwards to find it, and Johnny said it was all right for us—I mean for the people in the story—to do it, and Gaston said it wasn't."

"I see," the priest said. "And what happened in the story?"

Gwen hesitated. "We haven't got that far yet."

"And who had hidden this treasure?" the priest asked. "Someone who was in league with evil spirits? It seems to be a rather strange way of finding buried treasure."

"No," Gwen said. "As a matter of fact it was—we don't know who it was. Somebody here in Quebec City."

The priest laughed and stood up. "Well, then, I hardly think they would be advising a pact with the Devil. We have a few people who don't go to mass as often as they should, don't we, Gaston?" he said, patting Gaston's head. "But I hardly think that we have many people actually in league with the Devil." He looked down at the two boys, who were still sitting on the step. "Now, let us have no more fighting, eh? Is that agreed?"

They nodded.

"Good!" the priest said, and then, giving Gwen a

pat on the head, he continued on his way down the street.

They were silent for a while. Then Gaston said, "You know, he's right, the priest. The people in Quebec in those days were good Catholics, too. If any of them had hidden the treasure, I don't think they would have told anyone to say their prayers backwards to find it—not if it was anything to do with the Devil. You were right to begin with. I was crazy to think of that."

"Well, then, what does it mean?" Johnny said grumpily, not completely recovered from the argument yet.

"I don't know," Gaston said, "except that you're right: it can't mean that. We've got to try something else. If we can't make any sense of the message, we must try the map first. What do those six crosses mean that are on it?"

"We don't even know exactly where they're supposed to be on the island," Johnny grumbled. "There's nothing else marked on the map at all."

"I've got an idea," Gwen said. "I thought of this in bed last night, and then I forgot all about it again until now because of everything else that happened. Why don't we get a real map of the Island of Orleans, the way it is today, and compare it with the treasure map? Then we could at least see roughly whereabouts those crosses are supposed to be. That would give us some clue where to go and look."

The other two looked at her admiringly.

"Say, that's a good idea," Johnny said, in surprise, as though he never expected his sister to have good ideas.

"Why didn't I think of that? Where can we get a modern map of the Island from?"

"I think we have one in the house," Gaston said, getting up. "Wait here. I will go and look for it. I was right. She has a good head, this little Gwen."

9

The Lady with the Wheel

As soon as Gaston had gone into the house, Gwen turned to Johnny and said, "I wish you'd stop arguing with Gaston and fighting all the time. You're going to ruin everything. We wouldn't be on the track of the treasure at all if it weren't for him. And, anyway, I like him."

"That's because he keeps saying you're smart," Johnny said, and then, before Gwen could protest, he added quickly, "and, anyway, I like him too. I didn't start the fights. It was him. How was I to know he was so touchy about being French, and about religion and all that stuff? He's just got a chip on his shoulder. I don't care what he believes in as long as it doesn't stop us getting at the treasure."

"Well, just be careful, that's all," Gwen said. "Otherwise he might just quit altogether and then we'd be sunk."

"Huh, I reckon we could manage without him now," Johnny said. "If he's going to be so touchy all the time, he can go for all I care."

"Well, he can't go for all I care!" Gwen said, getting mad. "This treasure's as much his as it is ours and if you try to get rid of him, I'll . . . I'll . . ." Gwen frowned, thinking what she would do.

"All right, all right!" Johnny said hastily. "I don't want to get rid of him. What does everyone have to get so touchy about? I just meant he didn't have to stay with us if he didn't want to. Everybody always gets so mad!"

"Shush!" Gwen said, as the front door opened again and Gaston appeared, holding a map.

He came down the steps and sat between them, spreading the map out on the sidewalk without saying anything. Johnny looked at Gwen and then said, "Say, I'm sorry about that argument, Gaston. I didn't mean to say anything about your religion. I just meant that I didn't want to give up searching for the treasure, that's all."

"That is all right," Gaston said, staring down at the map. "It is my fault. I should not call you atheist. That is terrible."

"Oh, I don't care about that," Johnny said. "You can call me an atheist as much as you like. The important thing is—"

"But that is important," Gaston interrupted. "How can it not be important if someone calls you that? I should not have done it."

"Oh, come on, you two!" Gwen said. "There you go again. Why will you keep arguing? Let's look at this map. Johnny, give me that copy you made of the treasure map."

Johnny opened his notebook at the page where he had traced the map and handed it to her. Gwen put it down beside the new map and compared them.

"Turn it round until it's facing the right way," Johnny said quietly.

Gwen twisted the notebook until the two maps were facing the same way, lying side by side. It was still difficult to see where the crosses would be on the modern map, and Johnny had another idea.

"Give me the notebook back, Sis," he said. "I'll make another drawing of the treasure map and make it a bit bigger this time so that it'll fit over the modern one. Then we can see exactly where the crosses are supposed to be."

He made a second tracing of the map on another page of the notebook and then drew round the edge of it, making the outline larger. Then he tore the page out and handed it to Gwen. It fitted almost perfectly and they could see the outlines of the modern roads and villages on the island showing through the tracing of the treasure map. They all leaned over and examined it.

Each of the six cross marks on the treasure map was right in the middle of a modern village!

Gaston picked up the map and translated their names: "St Francis, St John, St Lawrence, St Catherine, St Peter, and Ste Famille. That's 'Holy Family' in English," he said.

"Well, that doesn't help us very much," Johnny said. "We can't search six whole villages! This is the craziest, most mixed-up treasure map I ever heard of."

"Do those names mean anything else, Gaston?" Gwen said, puzzling over the map.

"Well, they're the names of churches," Gaston said, "and the villages are named after them."

Gwen kept looking at the modern map, staring at the villages closely. Suddenly she said, "That's funny. These villages on the modern map have crosses in them too—little tiny ones. What do they mean?"

"Crosses? Where?" Johnny said, looking at the map closely. "Oh, those. Those are just the marks they put on maps to show where the churches are. Hey, wait a minute!" he said, after a slight pause. "You said those six villages were named after churches, didn't you, Gaston?"

"Yes, that's right. St Francis, St John—"

"Are they very old churches?" Johnny interrupted eagerly. "I mean, would they have been there two hundred years ago, when this treasure was buried?"

"I guess so," Gaston said. "These are all very old churches in the Island of Orleans, except St Petronille, and that isn't marked on our old map."

"That's it, then!" Johnny said excitedly. "That's what the crosses on the treasure map mean. We've been thinking all the time that they marked the spots where the treasure was buried, in fields or something, the way they do in books, but these crosses mean exactly the same as they do on a modern map. They mark the churches—the ones that were on the Island at the time the treasure was buried."

"Well, where does that leave us?" Gwen asked, puzzled.

"Well, the treasure must be in one of the churches."

"Yes, but which one?" Gwen objected. "There are six crosses on the map. How do we know which one the treasure is in? It might be in all of them, divided up!"

Gaston's lips had been moving silently and now, suddenly, he struck himself on the forehead. "*Tiens!*" he said. "What a fool I have been. The Lady with a Wheel, in the rhyme. It is St Catherine. St Catherine is the church we want."

"How do you know?" Gwen said. "What's that got to do with a lady with a wheel?"

"That is who she is, St Catherine," Gaston said. "St Catherine was one of the holy martyrs and she was killed by the Romans by being crucified on the wheel of a cart. I have been taught that in school, but I did not think of it in the rhyme until I saw the name of the church."

"How awful," Gwen said. "Why did they kill her on a wheel?"

"I don't know. It was just cruel, I suppose, but always in the statues and pictures of St Catherine she is shown holding a wheel, so you can tell who she is."

"Hey, I've heard that story," Johnny said. "You know that firecracker we have on Victoria Day that goes round and round when you pin it up and set light to it? That's called a Catherine wheel, and I remember Dad told me it was called that after some old saint who had been tortured on a wheel. But that wasn't a cartwheel. The wheel they used to torture people on was like a rack and they used to stretch 'em until they pulled all their arms and legs apart. I looked it up in the library once, when I was doing a composition for history class on tortures and executions."

"Yes, and you and Frank Reynolds tied me up and tried out what you said was a Chinese torture on me by dripping water on my head," Gwen said. "All you did was make me wet."

"That was because you yelled so much we had to let

you go, you baby," Johnny said. "You were supposed to stay tied up for weeks, with the water dripping on you. Then you would have gone slowly mad."

"I didn't want to do that when we had one madman in the family already," Gwen said, ducking quickly as Johnny swiped at her with the notebook.

"No, be serious," Gaston said. "If the treasure is really hidden somewhere in St Catherine's church, what do we do next? We could ride over to the Island this afternoon on our bicycles to see the place."

"That's no good," Johnny said. "You remember what the rhyme says. We've got to go there when the moon is full, to say our prayers backwards—or whatever it is," he added hastily, seeing the look on Gaston's face. "We don't even know what that means yet, but we might get some ideas if we go there when there is a full moon. Then there's that stuff about the serpent and going where none but the dead should go. We don't know what any of that means yet. If we go across to the Island at the right time we might begin to see how some of these things fit together."

"We know a lot more than we did when we started," Gwen said. "But how can we go over there when there's a full moon? That'll be in the middle of the night. We'd never be allowed to go out at that time. What reason could we give to Mummy and Daddy?"

"We won't tell them. We'll just sneak out of the house when they've gone to sleep. As long as we get back before they get up, they'll never know we've been away."

"We'd never get away with it," Gwen said. "We won't be able to get out of the house in the middle of the night without them hearing us. And if they catch us we'll be skinned alive."

"Why should they hear us?" Johnny said scornfully. "They didn't hear that burglar, did they? You're just scared."

"Burglar? What is this about a burglar?" Gaston said, and they suddenly realized that they hadn't yet told him about what had happened the night before. As they told him, he listened very seriously and then said, "This means we have got to work fast. If the others have got the map and message too, it may not take them as long to decipher it. We should try to go to the Island at once."

"The moon's certainly pretty full now," Johnny said. "It was shining through my window last night."

"I still don't think we can sneak out of the house in the middle of the night," Gwen said.

"Well, then," Johnny said. "Maybe we can stay out late. I'm pretty certain we could picnic out tomorrow afternoon if we wanted to. We could just be a bit late getting home."

"And stay out until it's moonlight!" Gwen said scornfully. "You're crazy. You know we'd have to be in by suppertime."

"All right, then," Johnny said, refusing to be beaten. "Maybe we can get permission to stay out for supper, and just be extra late getting home."

"No, I don't know where we could get invited for supper," he added quickly, guessing from the look in her eye what Gwen's next question was going to be.

"I could invite you for supper at my house," Gaston said. Then he shook his head. "But that's no good. When it was time for you to go home, my father would just drive you home and I would have to go to bed." He thought for a moment longer. "I know!" he said suddenly. "My grandmother! She lives by herself at Courville and she doesn't have a car. She would invite us for supper tomorrow for sure if I phoned and told her I had two English friends I wanted to bring to see her."

"Canadian friends," Johnny said firmly. "Where's Courville? Won't your father still want to drive us home?"

"No, I don't think so," Gaston said. "I have ridden back from there many times by myself after supper. If we tell him we want to ride out there on our bicycles tomorrow afternoon, he'll just let us ride home again by ourselves. We can make a little detour to the Island of Orleans on our way home. It's right on the way, almost."

"Where is Courville?" Gwen said, repeating Johnny's question. "Is it near enough for us to ride to on our bicycles?"

"Oh, yes," Gaston said. "It is just near the Island of Orleans, across the river. It is next to the Falls of Montmorency. It would be a good place to spend the afternoon anyhow. You must see the famous Falls before you leave Quebec, and the house of the father of the Queen Victoria, which is there, and we could swim in the river, and my grandmother, she is a wonderful chef. She will cook us good supper."

"It sounds wonderful," Gwen said. "Montmorency Falls! I've been wanting to see them."

"Are they as big as Niagara?" Johnny said. "We've seen Niagara."

Gaston shrugged. "They are not so big, wide," he

said, "but they are higher. I think they are much more good-looking. I have seen Niagara Falls too."

"Well this sounds fine," Johnny said. "The perfect solution. We'll just have to be late getting home, that's all. How long will it take us to get to St Catherine's church from there?"

"Not long," Gaston said. "We have just to go left across the bridge to the Island on our way back. It is just a few miles."

"You're forgetting that we've got to wait until the moon comes up," Gwen said quietly.

But for some reason the boys chose to ignore her.

10

The Graveyard Vigil

The next day everything went as planned. Gaston had phoned his grandmother that same evening and told her that he had two friends from English Canada who wanted to see Montmorency Falls, and, as he had expected, she had been very happy to invite them all to stay to supper. Both sets of parents had been consulted and had talked with each other over the phone, and it was agreed that Johnny, Gaston, and Gwen could ride out to Courville in the morning, taking their lunch with them, have supper with Gaston's grandmother, and then start for home.

"Anyhow," Johnny said to Gwen, when she kept on worrying about it, "that's what we're going to do. It's just that we're going to make a detour on the way back. Gaston's told you it won't take us long."

What no one except Gwen had admitted out loud was that although the detour might not take them long, waiting around for the moon to come up afterwards would. They had stayed out late before and got into trouble for it, but this adventure looked as though it might lead to a later bedtime and more trouble than they'd ever had.

Johnny and Gaston seemed determined to put that thought out of their heads until the time came when they would have to face the trouble. And at last, as the day at Montmorency Falls wore on, they won Gwen round to their way of thinking.

"Well, you know Mother," she said to Johnny, as she finally decided to give up worrying how late they would be. "If we're as late as I think we're going to be, she'll have the police, the army, and the fire department out looking for us."

But Johnny simply went on pretending to himself that they weren't going to be very late at all, as if some miracle was going to happen and they were going to have full moonlight while the sun was still shining.

They hung around for as long as they could at Gaston's grandmother's after supper, so that they shouldn't have to make too early a start for home, but finally the old lady insisted on their leaving while there was still some daylight to ride by. They kept telling her that they had lamps on the bicycles and that it was quite all right for them to be out after dark, but she wouldn't listen to them and began to threaten to phone Gaston's father if they didn't set off. And that was enough for them.

Still, they had managed to delay for so long that, when they left the house for the short ride to the bridge that connected the Island of Orleans with the mainland, the sun had already set. By the time they had crossed the bridge and were riding along the quieter, narrower island road, towards the village of St Catherine, it was dusk. It had become quite cool, with just the faintest whisper of a breeze in the tops of the trees. At the edge of the river, not far from the road, slight traces of mist were beginning to form. Overhead, in the darkening air, a few bats were flying, sweeping along the road in front of them or heading straight along it towards them and then darting up or to one side just in time to avoid them. They kept ducking as they rode along, afraid that one of the bats would collide with them.

They passed through one village, which Gaston told them was St Petronille, and then out into the country again, down the steadily darkening road. One or two cars passed them, but otherwise the countryside was perfectly quiet, with only the occasional lowing of a cow from across the fields, waiting to be milked.

Finally, Gaston stopped pedalling and pulled in close to the side of the road. He pointed ahead to where a small steeple showed through the trees.

"There is our church," he said. That is St Catherine just round the bend. I think we should leave our bicycles here and go on foot, over the fields, so that nobody sees us."

"Good idea," Johnny said, as he and Gwen dismounted. "We can hide the bicycles in the field behind the fence here."

No one had said anything, but it was obvious now that they were going to stay out until the moon had come up. Gwen shrugged. It was no use complaining now.

They took the Mouse out of his basket and let him run, then wheeled the bicycles down to a gate into the field next to them, laying them down on their sides in the grass, out of sight from the road. Then they set off across the fields, the Mouse running ahead of them, sniffing the ground excitedly at the thought of rabbits and other animals with burrows he could look into.

They crossed several of the long narrow fields, getting closer to the river as they approached the village, and then came to a little dirt footpath which led right into the village itself. The church was the very first building in the village from this direction, and the only thing between them and it now was the wide churchyard. Past the churchyard and the church they could see two or three small houses, widely separated and stretched out along the road, with lights shining in their windows.

"Well, the church is certainly lonely enough," Johnny said. "As long as we stay on this side of the churchyard, away from the road and houses, no one is going to see us. There's another thing, too. If the other people after this treasure have cracked as much of the message as we have, and come here tonight, they're certain to come by car. If we stay out of sight on this side of the church-yard we can see anyone who arrives by car, and they won't even know we're here."

"Let's move up closer then," Gaston said. "We are too far away here. We should make our base just this side of the churchyard wall. If we keep down below the wall, we will have all the cover we need while we are waiting for the moon."

They looked up at the sky which was already begin-ning to lighten in the east, where the moon would come up. Then they followed Gaston in single file along the dirt track. They turned off it at the churchyard wall, which was very low, only coming up to their hips, and walked along beside it in the field until they came to a huge elm tree at one corner of the graveyard.

"Let us stop here," Gaston said. "We can see from here across to the church, and the tree trunk will give us extra cover."

They dropped their knapsacks and looked around them. They were on the edge of a woodlot, which seemed to run all the way down to the river, a few hundred yards away. On the other side of them, between them and the church of St Catherine, was the churchyard, with its old crosses and headstones leaning in all directions over the small mounds of the graves. Among them, here and there, grew a bush or a small yew tree. It was quite dark now, except behind the church, where the sky was getting lighter as the moon rose.

"Golly," Gwen said, glancing at the crosses and headstones on the other side of the wall. "What a spooky place! Why can't we wait somewhere else?"

"Because this is the only place where we can watch the front of the church without being seen ourselves," Johnny said. "If we went round to the other side of the church, away from the graveyard, we'd be right out in the village street."

"Well, I'm going to watch this side, then," Gwen said, going round to the other side of the tree and sitting down with her back against it, facing the river. "You two can keep watch on the graveyard."

Johnny and Gaston both sat down by the tree, too, close to Gwen, but looking towards the church and the road, over the top of the low churchyard wall. Johnny called the Mouse softly and made him sit down beside them.

"There's nothing to be scared of in a churchyard, stupid," Johnny said as soon as he had got settled. "Everyone's dead so what harm can they do you?" He might not have been quite so sure if he had been alone, but with the other two beside him he felt quite brave.

"But do you remember what Daddy told us?" Gwen said. "Even in the old days this island was supposed to be haunted. People saw strange things here, and other people disappeared and were never seen again. You believe in ghosts just as much as I do, so don't pretend that you don't."

"Well, I just don't believe there are any ghosts in Quebec, that's all," Johnny said. "The only ones I've ever heard about were in Europe, in old castles and places, where people were shut up in dungeons and starved to death, or had their heads cut off, and things like that. There just aren't any ghosts here. They never allowed them to emigrate to Canada."

He laughed at his own joke, but Gaston said seriously, "In Quebec there is the *loup-garou*."

"The what?" Johnny said.

"The *loup-garou*. *Loup*—that means wolf, and *garou* —I don't know just what that means, but *loup-garou* is a man or an evil spirit that can change himself into a wolf at night, and he comes in search of men who have said bad things about the church, or who don't believe in God."

"What does it do to them?" Gwen said, moving round a little from her side of the tree.

"He attacks them and bites their throat and kills them," Gaston said.

"That's like the werewolf," Johnny said. He had read

dozens of ghost stories, and sometimes scared himself so badly reading them that he was afraid to go to bed.

"The where wolf?" Gaston had never heard the word.

"Yeah. He changes himself into a wolf at the full moon, and then prowls the countryside looking for victims. Hey, it's full moon tonight," he said, suddenly remembering. "That's why we're here."

And so they went on talking as the night wore on, Gaston and Johnny telling each other ghost stories they had read until they began to make Gwen's flesh creep.

"Oh, stop it, you two," she said finally. "It's bad enough out here in the dark among the gravestones, without you trying to scare us all with ghost stories."

And Gaston did suddenly change the subject. "There's one thing we have forgotten," he said. "When the moon comes up, we have got to be in the church. But we don't know if we can get in. The door will probably be locked already."

"Maybe there'll be a small window we can get in," Johnny said. "Or maybe they don't lock the church at all. Don't some people go into the church to pray at midnight sometimes?"

"Ah, but not at this time of year," Gaston said, shrugging. "That is only for special times, like Christmas, that we have the midnight mass. But I think I should go and scout now, to see how we can get in. When the moon is up, it will not be possible to walk around so much without being seen." He pulled a flashlight from his knapsack and stuffed it into his pocket. He had come prepared.

"Wait a minute," Johnny said. "Maybe I should go.

Or maybe we should toss up for it. Why should you take the risks?"

"It is not so much a risk while it is still dark," Gaston said. "And, besides, I am French and if anyone speaks to me I will attract not so much attention. They will think that I have some business to be here."

Johnny felt like protesting again, but he could see that it really was more sensible. Gaston would have much more chance of getting away with it if anyone caught him around the church. So he said simply, "Okay. We'll wait for you here. But don't be too long. There's more and more moonlight every minute."

Gaston climbed over the little churchyard wall and began moving cautiously in among the crosses and headstones towards the church. In a moment he had disappeared from sight. Gwen shivered. "Golly, he's brave," she said. "I wouldn't go through there by my-self."

"Why not?" Johnny said, feeling a little guilty. "I would." He knew that Gwen thought he was just boast-ing, and he wished he had some way of showing her that he had just as much nerve as Gaston.

Then they both jumped. The lights had suddenly gone on inside the church. Had Gaston put them on? No, that was ridiculous. He would never do that. But he must have arrived there just about the same time as they did go on. Or maybe their rivals had got into the church first after all, and had decided that they wouldn't wait for the moon to come up to start examining it. There was no telling what kind of risk they might take to get at the treasure first.

Johnny and Gwen sat in silence, straining their eyes and ears for some sound or movement from the direction of the church. But all remained silent.

And then, as Gwen turned round to watch the other direction again, she suddenly spoke in a terrified whisper that made Johnny's flesh creep.

"Look, Johnny—behind you. The light in the trees!"

11

A Mysterious Disappearance

Johnny turned round and looked, and there, sure enough, shining through the trees from the direction of the river was a small pale light, swaying from side to side slightly and moving up and down, as if motioning to them. At times it moved behind the trunks of trees and disappeared, and then reappeared again, still moving and swaying, but always in roughly the same spot.

"How long has that been there?" Johnny whispered.

"It just appeared suddenly as I turned round," Gwen said. "One minute it wasn't there, and the next minute it was."

"Well, it certainly can't be the light from a building, the way it's moving around," Johnny said. "It looks like a signal light of some kind. It might just be someone fishing down there. I'm going to see what it is. You stay here and hold the Mouse."

"Johnny, don't go!" Gwen said urgently. "You don't know what it might be. Remember what Daddy read us from that book about this island, how people went off after mysterious lights in the marshes and were never seen again. I know it sounds silly, but I don't like this whole business. Maybe we should never have come out here in the first place without letting anyone know what we were doing. We could disappear and no one would have any idea where we had gone to."

Johnny paused. There were enough creepy things about this affair to make him have doubts too, but if Gaston was brave enough to scout through the grave-yard to the church on his own, Johnny wasn't going to let himself be put off by a waving light.

"That's all a lot of nonsense," he said, trying to sound scornful. "I don't believe that stuff. And besides, I'm not going to follow the light anywhere. I just want to get up closer so that I can see what it is. Just sit here and hold the Mouse. I'll be back in a couple of minutes."

He got to his feet and began to move softly down the edge of the field towards the trees, then reached them and disappeared. The Mouse got to his feet and tried to follow him, but Gwen held onto him firmly and made him sit down again, putting one hand around his jaws to prevent him barking as he whined and struggled a bit. Then she put her arms round his neck for company and stared in the direction of the light, which still continued swaying gently, up and down, from side to side, disappearing, and then coming into view again.

All around her the night was perfectly still, except for the occasional screeching of some night bird, somewhere nearby, and the occasional zigzag flight of a bat past the tree over her head. There was no sound from the direction of the church, where Gaston had disappeared, nor from the direction of the trees, where Johnny had gone.

Then, suddenly, she jumped. The moon, which had

been rising for some time, suddenly came out into the open, over the roof of the church behind her, lighting up the landscape with its pale light and casting long shadows from the trees over the field in front of her. It was as if someone had suddenly turned on a light.

Now everything was ready, except that the other two seemed to have disappeared completely.

She wished they would come. Little fragments of her father's story about the Island and its strange lights; the message, with its mysterious instruction about saying your prayers backwards; Gaston's talk about evil spirits coming if you did, and about the *loup-garou* who prowled in moonlight; all came into her head in turn and made her hug the Mouse more tightly. They all seemed uncomfortably connected, somehow, and she began to wish she had gone straight home from Gaston's grandmother's, or that she had really tried to convince her parents about this whole thing from the very beginning. Maybe there were some things that ought to be left to adults. Suppose that Gaston and Johnny just didn't come back now. How long should she stay there waiting for them, before going off to report their disappearance at the nearest house?

She was uneasily aware of the churchyard behind her, with its leaning headstones and crooked crosses. Johnny was probably right about there being no harm in churchyards, but she wished she didn't have to sit right next to one in the middle of the night. She turned round now to look across it towards the church and her heart gave another jump. The lights in the church had gone out again and its windows were dark. Where was

Gaston, and what did this putting on and off of the lights in the church mean?

The Mouse gave a sudden violent squirm in her arms, and got loose. Before she could grab him, he was off down the edge of the field where Johnny had gone, towards the trees. Someone was there!

And then, thank heaven, it was Johnny, suddenly appearing out of the shadow of some bushes along the churchyard wall, treading silently on the soft grass. He bent down and scooped the Mouse up and then carried him back to where Gwen was sitting, her hand still on her mouth in alarm.

"Almost caught you napping that time," Johnny said. "If it hadn't been for the Mouse, I could have crept right up on you. You're not keeping a very good watch."

"I was keeping watch over towards the church," Gwen said indignantly. "The lights have gone out there now. I can't look in every direction at once, can I?"

Johnny turned and looked towards the church. The windows were completely dark again.

"No sign of Gaston?" Johnny said.

"No, and I don't like it," Gwen said. "He's been gone too long. He could have gone to the church and come back again a dozen times by now."

"Maybe we'd better go and look for him," Johnny said. "I'll go. You stay here with the Mouse in case he comes back another way while I'm gone."

"No!" Gwen's voice was so loud that Johnny shushed her in alarm. "Well, I'm not going to stay here alone again, and that's that!" Gwen said. "I'll come with you this time. And, anyway, you haven't even told me yet what that light was down there." She turned her head and looked towards the trees. "It's still there."

"It's a boat light," Johnny said. "That's why it's moving like that. Someone's hung a lantern of some kind on the mast of a small dinghy and tied it up to the shore. The water's making the boat move like that. Funny thing is, there's no one down there. They just seem to have tied the boat up and left it."

"D'you think it could be fishermen?" Gwen said. "They might have moved on somewhere else and left the light there so that they could find their way back to the boat easily."

"Could be," Johnny said. "They might be going along the shore setting night lines. But I didn't want to go too far to find out in case I bumped into them and they asked me what I was doing here. We might be trespassing, you know."

"Well, I don't care about that," Gwen said. "We're not doing any harm. What I'm worried about is Gaston. Johnny, something must be wrong. He's been gone so long."

"Okay. Let's go and find out," Johnny said. "Keep hold of the Mouse—no, here, give him to me and I'll carry him for a while. I don't want him running around and giving us away." He took the Mouse and hoisted him up comfortably in his arms. The Mouse yawned and licked Johnny's ear gratefully, making the most of this long rest for his short legs. It wasn't often that he got carried absolutely everywhere, and he liked it too much to complain. He settled down again with his head on Johnny's shoulder, looking drowsily at the scenery. The moon went behind a large cloudbank that had been building up from the horizon, and everything was suddenly dark.

"Now's our chance," Johnny said. "Before the moon gets out again from behind those clouds. Let's go around the churchyard, just in case Gaston ran into any trouble by going straight across it."

They skirted the churchyard wall, keeping low and moving quickly out of the field and down the little dirt track towards the village. When they were near the end of the track, Johnny crossed it, away from the churchyard wall, and took up a position behind a large elm tree. Gwen followed him. From here they could see clear across to the doors of the church and down the highway to the first houses of the village. Then the road curved away again and disappeared from sight, following the curve of the Island.

They stared across at the church, then at the churchyard facing it, then as far as they could see in either direction. There was no sign of Gaston, no sound or movement of any kind.

"I'm going to have to go out there and walk around," Johnny said finally. "He may have gone round to the back of the church, or he may be out there unconscious or lying tied up for all we know. The only way to find out is to go and look."

"Unconscious!" Gwen said. "What do you think's happened to him?"

"How do I know?" Johnny said impatiently, his own anxiety coming through. "I don't suppose he's unconscious at all—but something must have happened to him." He handed the Mouse back to Gwen firmly. "Now you stay here and watch me. I'm going to walk once

all the way round the church to look for him. You won't
be able to see me when I go round the back, but look
at your watch and if I don't come out round the other
side at the end of five minutes, you go down to that first
house down there and get help. Don't come after me,
d'you understand? Because if I don't come out from
behind the church in five minutes, there's something
wrong and you'll only be walking into it yourself if you
follow me. And if anything does go wrong, and I don't
come out again, don't waste any time. Run down to the
house as fast as you can, because whoever has got me
and Gaston is certainly going to try to get hold of you,
too, before you can get away."

Gwen felt a terrible fluttering sensation in her
stomach. Unconsciously, she squeezed the Mouse so
tightly to her that he gave a little yelp of protest.

"Johnny," she said. "Maybe, if it's as dangerous as
you say—maybe you shouldn't go at all. Maybe we
should both go down to that house now, before anything
else happens, and get help in looking for Gaston." She
began to think longingly of her warm bed at home, and
the comfort of having her parents asleep in the next
room, and she began to wish that they had never started
out in search of this terrible treasure to begin with. If it
had stayed buried in the ground for over two hundred
years, maybe they should just have left it there. Gaston's
talk about summoning the Devil and evil spirits came
into her head with a new seriousness. It was all very well
to sneer, but there were things in heaven and earth that
nobody understood. And didn't even serious scientists
believe in ghosts and hauntings and second sight and
thought transference and things like that, sometimes?

But Johnny wasn't giving her any time to persuade him of any of this. He patted her on the shoulder. "Okay, Sis. Keep your eyes open, and don't forget to look at your watch when I go out of your sight." And then he was off, walking boldly across the road, without any attempt at concealment now. He walked along the churchyard wall first, on the side nearest the church, looking over it at the crosses and headstones for any sign of Gaston, any marks of a struggle or anything that he might have left behind as a message for them. But there was nothing. Then he walked over to the front of the church, looking up at the carved golden statues of saints, standing in niches in the stone wall above the door. There, in the highest place of all, was St Catherine, holding at her right side a carved golden wheel—the Lady with the Wheel.

As Gwen watched, Johnny tried the door of the church, lifting the iron latch and giving it an experimental push and tug. It was locked. Gwen saw him shrug his shoulders and then start round the southwest corner of the church, to walk down the side she couldn't see, and then round the back, which she couldn't see either.

She looked at her watch nervously, shifting the Mouse to one side. Ten minutes to twelve. Golly! For a moment she was so startled at the time, and at the thought of what their parents would do to them when they got home, for staying out to this hour, that she forgot what she was doing. When she looked up again, Johnny was gone.

Already she had made a mistake. She hadn't actually seen him go round the corner, though surely nothing could happen to him while he was simply turning a corner. .... At all events, there was no noise, so nothing should have happened to him yet. But then, there had been no noise from Gaston either when he had disappeared.

She looked at her watch anxiously again and then up at the church. Not even a minute had passed! It was going to be the longest five minutes of her life. The words *Where none but the dead should go* flashed into her head, and she glanced uneasily at the graveyard. She began to think of saying her prayers, not backwards, but forwards, to ask that nothing should go wrong with Johnny, and then, to her immense relief, he came into sight again, round the back of the church. He looked in her direction and shrugged, holding his arms out from his sides slightly, as he began to walk along the north wall.

Gaston had disappeared from the face of the earth!

12

The Coiled Serpent

The moon came out from behind a cloud for a moment, bathing the whole scene in brilliant pale light. The silver roof of the church glistened, the golden statues above the door sparkled and the pale stone of the walls whitened. The whole building was like a jewel, shining against a pale velvet sky.

Then the moon went in again and the sinister quiet seemed to return, dropping over the church and the surrounding countryside like a shroud with the return of the darkness.

Johnny had kept close in to the wall of the church as the moon came out. Now he advanced into the open space in front of the doors, beckoning Gwen over. She put the Mouse down and ran to him.

"Not a sign!" he said, shrugging again as she came up. "There doesn't seem to be a stone out of place." He went over to the church doors again. "And the whole place is locked up," he said. "There isn't a door or a window open anywhere that we could get in. And we're certainly not going to break into the place."

He put his hand on the latch again to try it, and then,

suddenly, he jumped back as if he had got an electric shock. The handle had turned in his hand!

"It moved!" he whispered, standing back from it. And then, urgently, from inside the church they heard Gaston's voice.

"Hey, let me out of here, eh?" it said, close up against the inside of the door.

Johnny and Gwen looked at each other in amazement, and then began to laugh with surprise and relief. The Mouse came up and began to sniff the bottom of the door curiously, as if measuring the possibilities of crawling underneath it and joining Gaston.

"Never mind about laughing," Gaston said. "Let me out."

"How can we let you out?" Johnny said, talking close up against the door. "We haven't got the key."

"It's under the step outside," Gaston explained. "Look under the step."

Johnny looked down at the bottom of the door. There was a small wooden step that the door rested on, raised just about an inch from the ground. He bent down and slid his hand under it and his fingers closed over a large, cold, iron key. He drew it out and in a moment he had fitted it into the lock and turned it. The door opened inwards and he stumbled in with it as Gaston pulled on it urgently. Gwen and the Mouse crowded in behind them. They found themselves in a small dark vestibule, separated from the main body of the church by two swinging doors.

"What happened?" Gwen and Johnny burst out together as they grabbed hold of Gaston to see if he was real and all in one piece. "How did you get in here?"

"How did you know where the key was?" "How long have you been here?" "Why didn't you yell or something?"

"One at a time. I will tell you everything. But first we must get inside and lock the door again. Now we have got the key, we can get out again when we want to."

"Lock ourselves in?" Gwen said. "I thought you wanted to get out?"

"I meant open the door, that was all, and for you to get the key. It is inside we want to be, and somebody else has tried to get inside already."

"Somebody else? Who?" Johnny said.

"I don't know for sure, but two men. I think maybe the man from the store—the other voice I didn't recognize, but it had a French accent. It must have been the man who followed us. We never heard him speak before."

The lock on the church door was one of those old-fashioned ones which lock with the key both from inside and outside. Once it was locked, there was no way for anyone locked inside to get out if they didn't have the key. This was what had happened to Gaston. He told them that when he had left them and crossed the grave-yard to the church, he had been just in time to see the priest coming across to it from his house a little way down the road. Gaston had ducked down behind the churchyard wall and had seen the priest reach down and find the key under the step and then go into the church and turn the lights on.

"So that's what we saw!" Gwen said. "We saw the lights go on and wondered what had happened."

"When he had been inside for a little while, I thought that this was a good chance to have a look in there while the lights were on, and so I came over and came in. The priest was doing something in his room at the back of the church and so I sneaked in and looked round. But then, when the priest came out of his room at the back, I ducked down out of sight in one of the pews. I thought I would stay inside for a while after he was gone and see if I could find anything. I didn't know there was this kind of a lock on the door."

"What about these other guys you said tried to get in?" Johnny said. "When did that happen?"

"Well, when the priest had gone and locked the door and I suddenly realized I couldn't get out, I thought I had better stay by the door until you came to look for me. I knew you would decide soon something was wrong, and come after me. And I thought I would call you from inside the door. I sat on the bench here and waited, and I thought I heard you coming, but then I heard the voices and realized it was not you, so I kept quiet."

"What were they saying?" Gwen was wide-eyed.

"One of them tried the door, and when he found it was locked, he swore and said they had forgotten that, and would have to get something to open it with. The other man said, was there anything in the boat to do it with? And the first man said he didn't think so, they would have to see if they could find something in one of the farms in the village, like a crowbar."

"The boat!" Johnny said. "Then it's their boat down there! No wonder we didn't see anyone arrive by road." He explained to Gaston about the light and his discovery of the deserted boat.

"They must have been over here while you were looking at their boat," Gwen said. "What a bit of luck you didn't bump into them!"

"This means they'll come back here as soon as they've found something to break open that door with," Johnny said. "These guys are rough. They've already broken into our house. They're not going to let a little thing like smashing a church door stop them. So we may not have very long to work in. What if they arrive while we're here?"

"We can hide in the pews, the same as I did," Gaston said. "They will never know we are there."

"Okay. And now that we've locked the door, we'll have lots of warning when they start trying to get in. So let's get on with it."

"Get on with what?" Gwen said. "We don't even know what to do next."

The others looked at her. They didn't like to admit it, but she was right. By a lucky break they were inside St Catherine's church all right, but they knew no more about the rest of the riddle than they had when they started out.

"Well, we can at least look around the church," Johnny said finally. "Did you get any ideas while you were in here, Gaston?"

"No, not so far," Gaston said despondently. "But I didn't really look. I was so anxious to wait for you at the door, or to hear if the others came back."

They pushed in through the swinging doors now to the main part of the church, Gaston leading the way, and then stopped at the end of the aisle, looking around.

Gwen gave a little sigh of amazement. "It's beautiful!" she said. "Look at all that lovely gold carving!"

"That is French-Canadian woodcarving," Gaston said proudly. "Like those saints outside the church, over the door. Quebec is very famous for its wood sculptures. We have always had many fine carvers."

"It all looks so new and so beautifully painted," Gwen said. "How old *is* it?"

"Over two hundred years," Gaston said. "But the painting is new, of course. It is painted in gold paint in order to—how do you say?—in order to keep the wood strong."

"To preserve it," Gwen said.

They walked the length of the church, looking at the huge carved pulpit, covered with golden bunches of grapes and leaves, and at two flying gold angels, high up on the walls, blowing their wooden trumpets. The moon was behind clouds again, but the sky was bright outside and there was enough light in the church for them to see it all quite clearly.

They reached the front of the church and stopped at the communion rail, looking up at the altar and crucifix. Gaston bent his knee and crossed himself, as he had done when they first came in.

Johnny looked at him uneasily. "Gaston," he said. "You don't mind our being in here like this, do you? I mean, to look for the treasure and everything?"

"No. Why should I mind?" Gaston looked at him in surprise. "I want to find it too."

"But—" Johnny hesitated. "Well, I guess I didn't realize that the church would be so—well, so kind of,

holy to you. I thought maybe you would think that what
we're doing here was kind of unreligious."

Gaston smiled. "But we are not doing anything unreligious," he said. "Because the church is holy, that does
not mean that one cannot search for treasure there."

Johnny breathed a sigh of relief and sat down in the
front pew. Gaston and Gwen sat beside him, while the
Mouse rummaged around underneath.

"But I guess you're still against our saying our prayers
backwards?" Johnny said.

Gaston shrugged. "What good would it do? You
don't expect anything to happen, do you?"

Johnny made a wry face. "I guess not," he said.

They sat in silence for a moment. Johnny looked up
at the altar, frowning a little as he thought. Behind
them, the moon came out again and poured through the
side windows of the church, making it almost as bright
as day inside.

"Backwards you must say your prayers," he muttered.
"Not frontwards, but backwards . . . not frontwards, but
backwards." Suddenly he turned to Gaston.

"What would happen if you turned round and said
your prayers facing the other way, with your back to the
altar?"

Gaston looked at him curiously, and they all twisted
round in the pew to look back down the church. "Nothing, I suppose," Gaston said. "But no one ever does. Why
would you do that?"

"But that would be backwards, wouldn't it?" Johnny
said excitedly. "If we turned round and said our prayers
here, we'd be saying them backwards, wouldn't we?"

"Oui," Gaston said, getting interested. He turned

round and kneeled on the pew, facing the door. Johnny and Gwen did the same.

"That must be it!" Johnny said. "The message isn't telling us to say the words of our prayers backwards, but to face backwards when we say them, away from the altar!"

"Yes!" Gwen said, getting excited and clapping her hands together.

"Okay. Let's see," Johnny said. "What comes next?

> *Backwards you must say your prayers,*
> *In the Isle of Sorcerers,*
> *Where the worshippers all kneel,*
> *To a Lady with a Wheel...*

We've got it so far. What comes next?"

> *"Then, when summer moons are full,*
> *You will see a serpent coil ..."* Gwen said,

joining in. "Where? Can anyone see a serpent coiling?"

Gaston shook his head. "How could there be a snake in church every time the moon is shining?" he said. "It doesn't make sense."

"It must mean that the serpent is always here," Johnny said slowly. "And somewhere where the moon can shine on it on nights like this."

They looked down the church at the two shafts of moonlight that were pouring in through the windows now, striking across the floors and walls.

"What are they shining on?" Johnny said. "Let's go see."

All thoroughly excited now, they got up and walked quickly back down the church. The first patch of moonlight they came to, far down the church, was shining on the bare wall on the north side. They looked at the wall, then at the moonlit floor. Nothing.

They moved on to the second patch of moonlight, which was shining on the end wall of the church to the right of the swinging doors. It was shining full on the baptismal font and on a tall carved wooden panel on the wall behind it, the gold paint glittering in the light.

They crowded up to look at the panel. It was a carving of a slim apple tree, with a round bushy top, full of fruit.

"It is the tree in the Garden of Eden," Gaston said, in a whisper.

Johnny and Gwen nodded absently. It wasn't the tree that really interested any of them. What all their eyes were fixed on eagerly was the creature that was crawling up the tree in the carving, coiled round and round it and decorated in gold: a large, beautifully carved serpent, with its mouth open and its forked tongue flicking out.

13

Where None but the Dead Should Go

They stared at its glittering eyes in fascination for some moments, and then Johnny breathed, "That's it! We've found it!"

"You were right, in a way, Gaston," Gwen said, "when you told us that if we said our prayers backwards, the Devil would appear. This is the Devil, isn't it—the way he appeared as a snake in the Garden of Eden?"

"*Oui*, that's him," Gaston said. "And that is the tree of the knowledge of Good and Evil which grew in the Garden of Eden. He is coiled round it waiting for Eve."

"Well, this time it's going to bring us some good instead of evil," Johnny said, grimly, "if that treasure is at the end of it."

"The next thing is, you have to grasp its head," Gwen said. "The rhyme goes on:

Grasp its head, and come below,
Where none but the dead should go."

They edged past the font and looked at its head closely. "Well, here goes!" Johnny said, his heart beating with excitement. He stepped up close and put his hand around the head of the snake. It fitted it neatly, like the handle of a door—the idea occurred to Johnny at once—and he tried twisting it, first to the right, then to the left. Nothing happened.

He strained at it for a while, and then stopped and mopped his brow. His disappointment was written all over his face.

"Don't forget it may be very stiff," Gaston said, stepping into his place close to the carving. "Maybe it has not moved for two hundred years." He grasped the snake's head himself and began straining at it. His knuckles went white with the effort. And then, suddenly, and very slowly, the snake's head began to turn.

Gaston gave a gasp of triumph and then stopped for breath. Johnny took his place again. Fraction by fraction, the end of the serpent's head, where it joined the body, continued to move, squeaking painfully. Then, all at once, whatever was holding it gave way and it turned more easily, though still with a terrible squeak, until it had turned almost the whole way round and was quite disconnected from the body.

Johnny felt a weight move behind the carved panel and then, as he pulled on the serpent's head, the whole panel swung out and away from the wall, like a closet door.

The three of them gasped together. Behind the panel, where the solid wall should have been, the stone had been taken out to make a shallow recess, no bigger than a small closet. At the bottom of this, attached to the wall with small iron hoops, was a very old and rotten-looking wooden ladder, leading downwards, past the floor of the church, into the ground. The hole it ran into was just wide enough for a body to pass through, and as dark as a well. As Johnny leaned over to look down it, a draught of chill, dank air hit him in the face.

Behind the carved wooden panel which had swung out from the wall was a small movable beam of wood, attached to the snake's head on the other side, which turned when the snake's head was turned, and allowed the panel to open outwards like a door. When the panel was closed and the snake's head was turned back into its normal position, the beam of wood fell into place in a strong iron socket, set into the stone on the inside of the wall, and the panel was firmly locked in place. And when the snake's head was in position it fitted so closely to the body of the snake that the join merely looked like part of the criss-cross design on the snake's back.

It was an extraordinarily ingenious piece of work, which could have been done only by a master wood-worker—probably the same one who had done the amazingly skilful carving of the tree and the snake itself, as well as some of the other beautiful woodcarving in the church.

Johnny and Gwen and Gaston stood and looked at each other in silence. Then without a word, Gaston pulled out his pocket flashlight, and leaned over and shone it down the hole. The wooden ladder seemed to run down for about sixteen feet into the ground and then to reach a solid floor. About ten feet down, the narrow tunnel began to open out into what seemed, at the bottom, like a small, stone-walled chamber. But all they could see of it with the flashlight from the top was a small area of the floor near the foot of the ladder.

Gaston silently handed the flashlight to Johnny for him to hold, and put one leg over the wall into the recess,

reaching for the top of the ladder. He found it with his foot and tested it, supporting himself with his hands against the inside of the wall.

"It is not very strong," he said. "We will have to go carefully."

He began to climb down and in a short while had reached the bottom. Then he called out to Johnny to drop him the flashlight.

"I will hold it, while both of you climb down," he said. "It is quite safe if you come one at a time and walk very gently on the ladder."

"No, I'll hold it while Gwen climbs down," Johnny said. "And then I'll come down holding it. We don't want to drop it and break it or we'll be sunk."

He helped Gwen over the edge and held the flashlight carefully as she climbed down. As soon as she had reached the bottom, he transferred it to his left hand and prepared to go himself. There was a whimper from the floor. The Mouse had been watching the whole operation with intense interest. Here at last was a hole and it looked as if everyone else was going to climb into it, while he was left alone outside. It was more than he could bear. But there was no way for him to get up into the hole from the floor, and no way for him to get down it if he did get into it. Climbing down ladders was not one of his strong points. So . . . he whimpered.

Johnny looked at him, then at the hole, then at the flashlight in his left hand, and then at the ladder. He shook his head. "Not this time, Mouse," he said. "I'm afraid we might break the ladder if I tried to take you down with me. You sit here and stay on guard for us."

The Mouse gave a little groan and looked at him

reproachfully. Then, as Johnny cocked his leg over the wall into the tunnel and began to climb carefully down the ladder, the Mouse put his tail between his legs and began to look around for somewhere to sit and watch the hole where everybody else had disappeared.

Johnny climbed down the narrow tunnel carefully, holding onto the ladder with one hand and holding the flashlight in the other. The wood under his feet sagged and creaked protestingly at every step, and every moment he expected one of the rotted old rungs to break underneath him. But they held, and in a few moments he was at the bottom, being helped down by Gwen and Gaston.

He handed the flashlight back to Gaston, who swung it around them slowly in a circle.

They were in a little tunnel-shaped room about fifteen feet long by five feet wide. The floor was of earth, beaten down hard, but the walls were of roughly cut stone, curving up and in slowly to make a semi-circular roof about six feet above the floor. The ladder down through the wall of the church led in at one end and extended all the way to the ground.

The walls and the floor were damp with moisture and the whole room felt as cold as an icebox.

Gwen shivered. "It's as cold as the tomb," she said, and then, as she looked around her, "in fact, it's rather like a tomb. No wonder the rhyme says *Where none but the dead should go*."

"Of course it's cold," Johnny said, shivering a little himself. "We're about ten feet underground. It's like a root cellar that they used to use in the old days to keep their vegetables and drinks and stuff cold, before they had refrigerators."

Gaston swung the flashlight beam slowly round, but it showed them only the bare stone walls and the bare earth floor. Then, suddenly, at the far end of the tunnel, it rested on what they had at first taken for a rough bench of some kind, built against the end wall.

Now, as they looked more closely, they saw that it was actually three large, heavy-looking black leather trunks, which had been pushed back against the wall end to end.

For a moment, their hearts seemed to stop beating. Then, with a few quick steps, they reached the trunks and were bending over, looking at them.

Johnny tried opening the middle one, but it was locked. Gwen and Gaston tried to open the ones on either side of him too, but they were just as unsuccessful. All three of the trunks were locked, and there was no sign of a key.

"Well, there's only one thing for it," Johnny said. "I guess the owner isn't around to mind. We'll just have to try to break the locks. They're pretty old and rusty I bet; we shouldn't have too much trouble."

He raised one foot and gave the trunk in front of him a hefty kick against the keyhole. Immediately there was a slight crack, and the trunk bent inwards where he had kicked it, its catch broken. Johnny reached down and opened the lid, and on either side of him Gaston and Gwen aimed sturdy kicks at the trunks in front of them, with the same success.

The three lids were thrown up, and three pairs of eyes fastened on the contents.

"Golly!" breathed Gwen.

"Wow!" Johnny said.

"*Mon dit!*" Gaston added.

The three trunks were filled to the brim with silver.

Johnny reached down and picked up two large, heavy silver plates, weighing them in his hand. "These must be worth a fortune," he said.

The others started dipping into their trunks, pulling out trays and slim silver coffee pots, knives, forks and spoons, goblets and tankards, small silver statues and crucifixes, candlesticks, and other pieces of silver whose uses they couldn't even recognize, many of them elaborately patterned and decorated. There were even one or two pieces made out of gold.

Soon the floor beside them was piled high with objects they had taken out of the trunks to look at, and their hands were filthy from handling them.

"Holy mackerel!" Johnny said. "There's enough silver here to fill a small truck with! This candlestick must weigh at least a couple of pounds on its own!" He brandished it triumphantly.

"And this silver is really valuable," Gaston said. "These are antiques. Old Quebec silver is worth a terrific price. It is collected by museums and lots of wealthy people."

Gwen had started dipping into her trunk again, rummaging among the objects at the bottom. Suddenly she straightened up and said, "Look at this! Here's a roll of paper, with writing on it!" She unrolled it and looked at it and then handed it to Gaston. "It's in French," she explained.

Gaston took it and turned the flashlight directly on

it, closing the lid of his trunk again and sitting down on top of it to read the paper. He stared at it in silence for a while, his lips slowly moving. Johnny and Gwen waited impatiently.

"What does it say?" Johnny said at last, unable to wait any longer. "Not another secret message, I hope!"

"No," Gaston said, as he finished reading it, "but it explains what has happened. Listen."

He began to translate it to them slowly, tripping over some of the words.

"It says, *The ones who have signed this paper, who have been afraid since many years, all the time, that the English would come, and take this island and all the things we possess, have*—er—oh yes, *have taken the chance when this church of holy St Catherine was built again the last time to*—*construire*—that's, let's see, *to build a safe and secret place where we could put our things in the case of danger. All the things that we cannot easily take with us, carrying them, we will leave here until the enemy is at last conquered and retreats; if not, until we can get them again safely. There is no one but us three and Monseigneur de Brébeuf who knows about this and he*—what is this?—ah yes, *and he cannot speak of it.* Then it ends, *God preserve King Louis and the New France* and there are these three signatures."

Gaston peered at the writing in the light of the flashlight, trying to decipher them: *"Louis Mesnil, Seigneur de Vermet; Vincent Carbonneau, Seigneur de Ste Catherine* and *Father Joseph Lepage, who is priest of this parish."*

"Who are they?" Johnny said. "What's a *seigneur*?"

"Those are the landowners," Gaston explained. "In the French days, the land was divided up into *seigneuries*, which were owned by a *seigneur* or lord. They controlled the farmers and peasants and some of them were very rich."

"So that's it," Johnny said. "And I guess when Wolfe came with his fleet in 1759, these *seigneurs* hid the stuff here and escaped to Quebec."

"*Oui*," Gaston said. "Everybody fled from the Island before the English landed. They would not have been able to take everything with them. Only money, maybe, and small things, like jewellery."

"I wonder why they never came back . . ." Gwen said. "After all, the British let everybody else come back after they had captured Quebec. They would have had plenty of time to get the treasure up again secretly."

"What do they mean by saying that only the three of them know about it, and *Monseigneur de Brébeuf*, who cannot speak? Does that mean the book we found the map and message in?" Johnny said.

"I guess that is it," Gaston said.

They sat on the three trunks without speaking, looking at the pile of old silver on the floor.

"You know, it's a funny thing," Johnny said, breaking into their thoughts. "We've been so busy tracking down this treasure and so caught up in how we were going to beat those other guys to it, that we've never really thought about what we were going to do with it when we found it. It's not really ours, is it? I guess it belongs to the church or something."

Gwen nodded slowly and Gaston said, "That's right. If it doesn't belong to the church, it will probably belong to the province of Quebec and go into the Provincial Museum at Quebec City. But the people who find treasure always get paid a large part of the value of what they find, a third, I think, or maybe a quarter."

"Well, I certainly won't complain about that!" Johnny said, looking at the size of the pile. "This stuff's going to be worth a fortune."

"You know, there might still be some descendants of the people who hid this alive," Gwen said. "In that case . . ."

But she never finished, for suddenly there was a sound of furious barking from the church above. The Mouse was sounding the alarm!

14

Playing for Time

Johnny moved to the other end of the underground chamber and listened at the bottom of the ladder. Now, mixed with the Mouse's furious barking he could hear another and fainter sound: the noise of protesting and splintering wood. Someone was forcing open the church door!

As Gaston and Gwen joined him at the foot of the ladder, Johnny said, "It's them! We've got to get that secret panel closed before they get in!" And he started up the ladder, climbing quickly and clumsily.

"Watch out for that ladder!" Gwen called in alarm. "It's going to break!" But the ladder held up until Johnny got to the top of it, though it shook and creaked mightily as he rushed up it. It was what happened at the top that proved the last straw. The secret panel was open into the church, just the way they had left it, and Johnny had trouble reaching it from the top of the ladder to swing it closed. Instead of getting off the ladder and out into the church, he tried leaning across from the ladder to grab it that way. This took his arms away from the ladder, where he had been supporting some of his weight with his hands, and threw all his weight suddenly on his two feet on the top rung of the ladder. He managed to grab the wooden panel all right, and to close it with the wooden bar, but the sudden strain was more than the old wood of the ladder could take. The top rung broke under him, and then the second and third and fourth as the full weight of his feet fell right down on top of them. He was halfway down the tunnel to the secret chamber before his body became wedged against the narrow stone walls and he was able to stop himself from falling. He lowered himself gingerly onto the next unbroken rung, feeling his scraped knees and elbows beginning to smart, and then, as Gaston shone the flashlight anxiously from below, he looked up. The top four feet of the ladder were completely wrecked. Every rung above the one he was standing on was broken, and he was about seven feet away from the bar on the secret panel. There was no way of reaching it. They were trapped inside!

Johnny climbed slowly down the rest of the ladder into the underground chamber, where Gaston and Gwen were brushing themselves clean of the shower of broken wood and pieces of rock that had fallen down on them.

"What happened?" Gwen said, wiping some small pieces of rock and wood dust off her tongue. "I told you to be careful."

Johnny told them. For a moment they didn't seem to realize what he was saying.

"You mean we're trapped in here?" Gwen said at last. "We can't get out?"

"Not unless we can attract someone's attention in the

church and tell them how to get us out," Johnny said quietly.

"But we know who is in the church right now," Gaston said. "We don't want to attract their attention."

"They may find us anyway, before too long," Johnny said. "They've obviously solved this much of the message, and if we could figure out the rest there's no reason why they shouldn't be able to."

"But, anyhow, they can't get down here," Gaston said contentedly. "Now that the ladder is broken, even if they find the snake's head, there is nothing they can do, unless they have got ropes and all kinds of stuff. Maybe we cannot get out, but they cannot get in, too."

"That's right," Johnny said. "So all we've got to do is stay put."

"But how long?" Gwen said anxiously. "It's awfully cold in here. How long are we going to have to wait until someone else comes into the church that we can call to?"

"Tomorrow morning, I guess," Gaston said. "When the priest comes in to say the mass."

"Well, what time will that be?" Gwen said, not at all reassured.

"Oh, I don't know. It's different in different places. Maybe six or six-thirty."

"Six or six-thirty! Why, that's hours yet!" Gwen looked at her watch. "It's only twelve-thirty now. We'll freeze to death."

"No, we won't," Johnny said. "It's not that cold. We just have to keep moving—keep walking round and round the room here and banging our arms." He began walking up and down demonstrating, the way he tried to keep warm in the winter sometimes on the way to school.

Suddenly Gaston held up his hand to stop him. "Hold it! Keep quiet for a minute. Listen!" He was standing at the foot of the ladder, his head cocked on one side to hear better.

Johnny and Gwen walked back and joined him at the foot of the ladder. "What is it?" Johnny said. "I don't hear anything."

"That is it. That is what I mean. The dog has stopped barking."

Johnny and Gwen's faces became serious. It was true. There was no sound of the Mouse. And knowing the Mouse, that could only mean one thing. Someone had stopped him barking, in the only way he could be stopped by anyone except the Matthews family, by force.

"Oh, poor Mouse," Gwen said, with her hands to her mouth. "We should have brought him down here with us. What have they done to him?"

"I hope they didn't hit him with their crowbar," Gaston said seriously. "They must be pretty desperate by now."

"Oh no!" Gwen gasped.

"Quiet a minute!" Johnny was listening at the foot of the ladder now and he motioned to them to keep still. "There's someone up there at the top of the tunnel. I can hear them banging about on the wall. They must be testing to see if it's hollow."

Gwen and Gaston stopped talking, and now the sound of several distant wooden thuds came to them from up above, then a sudden squealing noise.

"Get back!" Johnny whispered. "Over by the treasure chests. Gaston, put your flashlight out! They've found it. They're opening it up!"

Gaston snapped off his flashlight and they crowded back to the far end of the chamber among the silver, kicking several pieces with their feet in the pitch darkness.

"Keep absolutely quiet!" Johnny murmured. "Don't let them know we're here."

They pressed back against the cold damp wall, out of sight of anybody up above, and even tried to breathe more quietly. To them the beating of their hearts and the pounding of the blood in their ears sounded almost like an express train passing through.

A pale light began to show at the bottom of the ladder, as the panel at the top was slowly opened. They looked at each other's grey faces in the new light and waited.

They heard muffled words at the top of the tunnel: "Ladder . . . wood's just broken . . . down there . . ." And then they saw the shadow of someone leaning over the opening at the top to look down. A flashlight came on and bright yellow light flooded around the foot of the ladder. Then a voice came to them hollowly, echoing in the tunnel, but unmistakable—the man from the antique shop.

"All right now, we know you're down there. Are you going to come out quietly with whatever you've found, or do we have to come down there and get you? I warn you, you'll be sorry if we do."

Johnny looked at the others and clamped his mouth firmly, and they immediately understood his signal.

There were several moments of terrible silence, and then the voice spoke again.

"I warn you, we can get you out of there whenever we want to, one way or another. For instance, we can smoke you out. Look."

There was the scratch of a match at the top and a sudden flare of light. Slowly a flaming twist of paper drifted down the tunnel and burnt itself out on the floor, filling the chamber with a faint smell of smoke. They looked at each other in alarm.

"Now, why not be co-operative?" the voice went on. "It'll be so much more pleasant for you. I'll give you one minute to make up your minds. We haven't got much time. That blasted little dog of yours is probably already waking up the whole Island with his barking."

The flashlight snapped out and there was silence. The man seemed to have gone away from the top of the tunnel.

Gwen let a little sigh of relief escape. "The Mouse got out," she whispered. "He's all right."

"Yes, but that is not much help," Gaston murmured. "The man is right. He can smoke us out of he likes. What are we going to do?"

"Play for time," Johnny said. "I don't know what good it'll do, but it's our only chance. The Mouse may wake someone, and they may notice there's something going on. Anyway, we haven't got any choice."

He stepped out of hiding and stood underneath the ladder. "All right," he shouted, looking up. "You win. But we can't come out anyway. The ladder's broken."

The man reappeared at the top and snapped the flashlight on again, shining it down into Johnny's eyes.

"Very sensible," the man said. "Don't worry. We'll get you out. But first, let's have whatever you've found down there."

"There's nothing here," Johnny said. "It was all a hoax."

The man laughed softly. "So, you're not going to co-operate," he said. "Very well, we'll burn you out." He held out a twist of newspaper for Johnny to see, and produced a book of matches.

"Okay! Okay! You win," Johnny called up. "There's a lot of old silver down here. But we'll have to bring it up the ladder as far as we can piece by piece. That ladder's going to collapse if we put too much weight on it."

"We can do better than that," the man said. "We'll lower you a sack on the end of a rope. You fill it, and we'll pull it up. When you're finished, we'll pull you out—if you've been co-operative."

Some hopes! Johnny thought. Once they've got what they want, they can lock us in here again for the night, while they make a clean getaway.

The man came back to the top of the tunnel, and soon a burlap sack snaked down on the end of a strong rope. Johnny dragged it into the chamber close to the silver and motioned to Gwen and Gaston. "Come on," he said quietly. "Let's fill it. But make it nice and slow."

Then he walked back to the bottom of the shaft. "What d'you think you're going to do with this stuff, anyway?" he yelled up. "It doesn't belong to us, you know."

The storekeeper leaned over again and looked down. "It may not belong to you," he said. "But it does belong to me. You found the book that led you to this in my store."

"That's right, we did find it," Johnny yelled back, "even though you tried to swindle us out of it after we'd paid for it. If we hadn't found it, it'd still be there now, going mouldy in that old chest. You've got less right to the treasure than we have! It belongs to the church."

"Stop your yapping and get that bag loaded," the man said fiercely. "We haven't got all night to waste. Whether it's yours or not, or the church's or not, it's going with us now. Get on with it."

"How long d'you think it's going to take the police to catch up with you?" Johnny said, ignoring his order. "You've burgled our house, smashed open the church door, and now you think you're going to get away with all this silver. Unless you're thinking of murdering us you won't be able to stop us talking when we get out of here, you know."

"I will murder you, you little brat, if you don't get on with loading that bag," the man snarled. "We'll be a long way away by the time you get out of here in the morning. D'you think we're fools?"

Gwen and Gaston had finished filling the first bag with silver now, and reluctantly Johnny watched the man haul it up to the top. As the pieces clattered out onto the floor of the church above, they heard the men exclaim excitedly. Immediately the sack and rope snaked down again.

They had filled half a dozen bags and sent them to the top, working as slowly as they dared, when there was a sudden excitement at the top of the tunnel where the men were hauling the silver into the church. Johnny had just added the last piece to another load and was looking unhappily at the disappearing pile of silver in the underground chamber, when the man who had started pulling on the rope dropped it again. Johnny heard a rapid and angry exchange of words above his head.

"That blasted dog!" the storekeeper said. "Keep quiet and they may go right past."

Johnny beckoned to Gwen and Gaston and they came and stood with him at the foot of the ladder, listening and looking upwards.

Faintly, but growing gradually louder, they heard the familiar sound of the Mouse's barking, and then with it the sound of voices shouting.

Suddenly, the voices became quite clear and the barking rose to a peak.

"Come here, you fool!" the shopkeeper exclaimed at the head of the tunnel. "Keep away from that door. You'll lead them right here!"

"It's the police!" they heard the other man exclaim. "There's a police cruiser on the road outside!"

Then the door closed and the outside voices became muffled again, though the sound of the Mouse's barking was still loud and close by. But in the underground chamber they had already heard enough and were looking at each other in astonishment.

"That was Dad!" Johnny said to Gwen in amazement. "How on earth did he get here?"

"That was my father, too," Gaston said. "I recognized his voice."

They stared upwards, straining to hear more, and then, after a moment's silence, there was a crash as the church door was thrown open violently and then a sudden scuffle and argument inside the church as several people seemed to burst in at once.

"No you don't!" they heard someone grunt. Then, "Look out! Grab him before he gets away!"

Then there came a vicious outburst from the store-keeper: "Blast you! Keep your hands off me!"

Another scuffle, a crash, then silence—except for the Mouse, who had been barking continuously through-out.

"Hey, Dad!" Johnny yelled up the shaft of the tunnel towards the light. "We're down here! Can you get us out?"

A couple of heads poked over the opening of the tunnel, at the top, and then Mr Matthews's voice came down to them.

"Are you all right? Is Gaston with you?"

"Yes, we're all right," Johnny yelled back. "He's here with us. Can you get us out?"

Mr Matthews's head withdrew and now Gaston's father leaned over and shouted a few words down at his son.

"Now we are for it!" Gaston said, turning to Johnny as soon as his father had finished. "They are—how do you say?—hopping mad. They have been looking for us since several hours, with the police as well."

A short discussion had been taking place at the top of the tunnel, and now another head poked itself over the side and looked down at them. It was wearing the peaked cap of a police office.

"Is there any more of this silver down there?" a voice said, with a strong French accent, and when Johnny called up that there was, the voice spoke down at him again.

"Okay, then you might as well send it up first, before we get you out."

The trio in the treasure chamber set to work with a will to load the rest of their find, and within a very few minutes the last two loads of silver had been packed into the burlap bag and hoisted to the top of the shaft.

Then, one at a time, Gwen, Johnny, and Gaston climbed to the top of what was left of the ladder and were hauled out the remaining few feet into the church by strong hands.

15

The Mouse Trap

They blinked a little in the full light of the church after the darkness of the tunnel, then looked around them. The Mouse came bouncing up, barking gleefully and jumping up at Johnny, Gwen, and Gaston in turn, until Gwen swept the dog off his feet and hugged him in her arms.

Mr Matthews and Mr St Hilaire, Gaston's father, were still in the church with one of the policemen, who was examining the pile of old silver on the floor and the opening of the secret tunnel. There was a little, awkward silence at first between the three treasure-hunters and their fathers, but then Mr Matthews and Mr St Hilaire began beaming quite unlike parents who were supposed to be violently angry and started grabbing their children's arms and shaking them a little, as if to be sure that they were quite all right, with no bones broken. Then a torrent of questions and answers broke out on both sides.

Johnny was the first to get in the question that he, Gwen, and Gaston were most curious about.

"But how did you find us, Dad?" he said. "How did you know we were over on the Island to begin with?"

"We guessed that much," his father said. "After all that fuss you'd been making about the Isle of Sorcerers and Montcalm's treasure, it seemed fairly certain where you'd gone when we discovered that you had left Gaston's grandmother's house and hadn't arrived anywhere else. Your mother's cruising around somewhere else on the Island, by the way, with Gaston's mother. They're in another police car. She was the one who started it all. You know how she worries. As soon as it got dark she was phoning Gaston's mother to see if you'd arrived there, and then, later, when Gaston's grandmother was called and reported that you'd left a couple of hours before, your mother nearly raised the roof.

"When it got to be very late and you still hadn't shown up, she insisted on calling the police. We guessed at where you might have gone and they brought us over to the Island to cruise around and look for you."

"But, Dad," Gwen broke in. "How did you know exactly where we were? I mean, in this church?"

"You can thank the Mouse for that," her father said, reaching over and scratching the dog's head. "We were driving along slowly about a mile from here when we saw him in the headlights, heading for home as if his tail was on fire. I got out of the car to call him and as soon as he saw me he turned right round and started high-tailing it back here with us behind him. Mr St Hilaire and I got out of the car to follow him and call out for you, in case you'd had an accident somewhere, and he led us straight to the church door and inside."

"Good old Mouse," Gwen said, giving him an extra squeeze. "He ought to get a medal."

"*Oui*, I think we give him a silver collar," Gaston said, grinning broadly. "Or, no—maybe a special little silver mouse trap because of the way he caught the crooks."

"A silver mouse trap!" Johnny said, laughing out loud. "That's what we'll give him! To hang from his collar to commemorate the way he caught the crooks."

"By the way, where is that guy we've never seen?" Gwen said, looking round. "He didn't get away, I hope."

"He didn't get away," the policeman said, coming over from the pile of silver which he had been examining. "We've got him outside in the car. I want you to come outside and see if you can identify him."

"We'd certainly like to see his face," Johnny said, "though I don't think we're going to be able to identify him. I don't suppose we ever saw him before in our lives."

As they all bundled out of the church door, they saw the second police cruiser drawing up and parking alongside the first, which had reported what had happened over the radio. As soon as it stopped, Mrs Matthews and Gaston's mother almost fell out of the rear doors in their eagerness to examine for themselves the exact state of their children's health. It was a few minutes before the policeman could get hold of them again to take them over to his cruiser to identify the prisoners.

But when they reached it, they got a severe shock. There was only one prisoner, the storekeeper, sitting in the back seat, no longer smiling, his wrists handcuffed together.

"Yes, we know him," Johnny said eagerly. "He's the one who owns the antique shop. But where's the other one?"

"The other one?" the policeman said. "What other one? There was only one man in the church when we got there."

"No, there was another one," Gaston said, looking round. "He is the one we have never seen; the one who has been helping this man."

"What about this?" the policeman said, leaning into the car and speaking to the storekeeper. "Where's your friend?" But the storekeeper just scowled and looked away.

"I know!" Johnny said. "The boat! He must have slipped out of the church without your noticing him and headed down for the boat." He pointed back across the churchyard towards the river. "It's moored down there. We saw it earlier."

There was a hurried conversation among the four policemen who were now on the scene, and two of them set off immediately for the river, running, with flash-lights in their hands.

But ten minutes later they were back with the group still gathered round the cruisers outside the church. They were alone.

"The boat's still there, all right," one of them said, "with the light on it. But there's no sign of a man. Are you sure there was a second one?"

"Of course we're sure," Gwen said. "They've been in it together all along. We heard them talking in the church."

Everyone now turned to watch the arrival of the

parish priest, who had been roused from his bed by one of the policemen to come and take charge of things at the church. As he walked towards them along the road from his house, Gaston suddenly slapped his knee.

"I know!" he said. "The pews! Where I was hiding from the priest. He must be hiding there, the other one. You would never see him if he kept down and was quiet."

He turned and ran the few paces into the church with Johnny and Gwen and all the rest of the group behind him. As soon as they were inside, they split up, one group going down each of the three aisles, looking along the lines of the pews.

It was Gaston who found him, about a third of the way down the church, lying full length on the floor between two of the rows of benches, waiting for the right time to escape. And as Gaston saw him and gave a shout, the man sprang at him and pushed him roughly aside, knocking him full length on the floor.

But he only got a few steps farther. Gaston's father, who was right behind his son in the centre aisle, swung at the man and connected, doubling him over, and then swung again, hard to the jaw. The man gasped and sat down, his face full in the light for the first time. Now it was the treasure-hunters' turn to gasp.

It was the attendant from the museum!

It was a little later, when the two families were sitting together at the priest's house, having hot chocolate and sandwiches, that the full story finally came out.

The owner of the antique store had remained silent, unwilling to tell the police anything. But before they had both been taken away into Quebec City, under arrest, his partner, the museum attendant, had talked enough for both of them.

The reason Johnny, Gaston, and Gwen had failed to recognize him before, they realized now, either when they had caught a glimpse of him looking into the antique store window or following them up the steps, was that the first time they had seen him at the museum he had been in uniform, dressed completely in blue, with a peaked cap. And as anyone who has had a relative in the armed forces knows, there's nothing like a uniform to change the looks of a man. They had sensed something familiar about him, but they had never got a close enough look at him to recognize who he was.

It was true, as Johnny and Gaston had suspected, that he had overheard them talking from the back room of the store, where he lived with his friend, the owner. And it was he who had gone round to the front of the store, through the back alley, to warn his partner not to let them have the book they were so interested in. He had not managed to hear all the details of what they had found in it, but enough to let him know that it was in some way connected with the treasure. It had been sheer bad luck that had made them go into this store on the one day of the week which was his day off from work, just as it had been sheer bad luck that had made them run into him to begin with, on that very first day when they had visited the museum.

But whether he had been in the store or not would probably have made very little difference after that first fatal meeting at the museum. For from that time on, the store owner had been ready for them, warned by his partner.

For the fact was that these two had already been searching for some time for some clue to the whereabouts of Montcalm's treasure, which they had come to believe really existed. It was for this reason that the storekeeper had made such a collection of old maps and was always asking customers in his store for more. It was for this reason, too, that his partner had finally managed to get himself a job as an attendant at the Provincial Museum, so that they could have completely free use of all its collection of old Quebec maps and documents. These the attendant would remove secretly from the museum's collection and take home, so that he and his partner could study them at their leisure. Then he would smuggle them back in again, before they could be missed, though the temptation to keep some of the more valuable ones had been too much for the two men and—as the museum was to find later when it examined its collection—these had disappeared entirely, sold to unknown collectors for high prices. So the police suspicion of the storekeeper as a dealer in stolen goods was proved too.

Naturally, as soon as Johnny and Gwen had turned up at the museum asking about Montcalm's maps, and Gwen had made some slight remark about the treasure, the attendant was on the alert, anxious to find out who they were and exactly how much they knew.

And it was here that Gwen had fallen into his trap, as she now ruefully admitted. When he had asked them to sign the Visitors' Book, it had been in the hope that this would give him some clue as to who they were, but Gwen had done better than that. She was just the girl he needed, for whenever she wrote her name and address on anything, including her school books, she was one of those people who put in everything, right down to "Canada, North America, the Northern Hemisphere, the World, the Universe, Space." And so, whereas Gaston had simply written the word Quebec after his name, and Johnny had just put down the name of his home town, Gwen, wanting to write something different from Johnny, had written out their full Quebec City address, as the man had seen to his great satisfaction before he closed the book.

So there had been no need for him to follow them home in a taxi to find out where they lived, as Johnny had suspected after the burglary. When he had discovered, by following them and listening to their conversation at the top of the steps, that they had got the map and message out of the shop after all, he had been content to let them go because he already knew their address.

He and his partner had suspected some trick when they had examined the book of sermons while the trio were away getting the extra money they needed. They had been able to find nothing in the book themselves and had decided that to be safe they had better both switch the books and follow the three youngsters for a while to see what they did. And as the youngsters were less likely to recognize the museum attendant, he had done the following.

In their tour of the antique shops of Quebec City, they had been bound to come to this one sooner or later and, as they realized now, it was no wonder that the owner had seemed to know all about them as soon as they had walked in the door. He had! But it had come as much as a surprise to him as it had to Johnny, Gaston, and Gwen when the treasure they had stumbled on turned out to be not Montcalm's at all, but somebody else's.

The only remaining mystery was solved for them by the parish priest. It was no wonder, he told them, that Father Lepage and the two *seigneurs*, Louis Mesnil and Vincent Carbonneau, had never come back for their treasure. The boat they were sailing on, in their flight from the Island of Orleans, had been overcrowded with refugees and had foundered in the St Lawrence. All three had drowned in the icy water, leaving only the map and message in the book of sermons to show that there ever had been a treasure.

And, as Johnny added, if they hadn't been searching for a different treasure entirely, it might never have been discovered at all.

As for General Montcalm's treasure itself, that may be there still. Certainly nobody has found it yet.

THE SECRET CIRCLE

1. THE MYSTERY OF MONSTER LAKE / David Gammon
2. THE RIDDLE OF THE HAUNTED RIVER / Lawrence Earl
3. THE LEGEND OF THE DEVIL'S LODE /Robert Collins
4. THE SECRET TUNNEL TREASURE / Arthur Hammond
5. THE MYSTERY OF THE MUFFLED MAN / Max Braithwaite
6. THE CLUE OF THE DEAD DUCK / Scott Young

General Editor   ARTHUR HAMMOND